浅見洋子 日英詩集

独りぽっちの人生(せいかつ)

東京大空襲により心をこわされた子たち

訳　岡和田晃

Yoko Asami's Poetry Collection In Japanese & English
The Struggling Children of the Tokyo Air Raids

English translation by Akira Okawada

コールサック社

浅見洋子 日英詩集

独りぽっちの人生(せいかつ)
―― 東京大空襲により心をこわされた子たち

目次

Yoko Asami's Poetry Collection In Japanese & English

The Struggling Children of the Tokyo Air Raids

Index

English Translation by Akira Okawada

第一章　独りぽっちの人生 ――六歳の智恵子

- 夕　日 …………………………………… 8
- 子　守 …………………………………… 14
- 差　別 …………………………………… 14
- 結　婚 …………………………………… 16
- 祈　り …………………………………… 18

第二章　こわれた心 ――一歳の幸一

- 別　れ …………………………………… 24
- 子犬のシロ ……………………………… 26
- こわれた心 ……………………………… 30
- 幸一の戦後 ……………………………… 32

第三章　うばわれた魂 ――三歳の由美子

- 叔母の背 ………………………………… 38
- 伯母の家で ……………………………… 40
- 恐　怖 …………………………………… 42
- 声 ………………………………………… 46
- 二行の命 ………………………………… 48

第四章　三ノ輪の町で ――八歳のマサヒロ

- 空　襲 …………………………………… 54
- 母ちゃんと ……………………………… 58
- 三ノ輪の町 ……………………………… 62
- ヒロポン ………………………………… 64
- アルコール依存症 ……………………… 66
- 家庭内暴力 ……………………………… 70
- 別れに …………………………………… 76
- マサヒロの心は ………………………… 78

Chapter 1 A Sole, Daily Life; Chieko Was Six-Year-Old

- Sunset 9
- Babysitting 15
- Discrimination 15
- Marriage 17
- Pray 19

Chapter 2 The Broken Heart; Koichi Was One-Year-Old

- Separation 25
- Shiro, the Puppy 27
- Broken Heart 31
- Koichi's Post-War 33

Chapter 3
The Swallowed Soul; Yumiko Was Three-Year-Old

- Aunt's Back 39
- At Her Aunt's House 41
- Terror 43
- Voice 47
- Two Lines of Life 49

Chapter 4 At Minowa Town; Masahiro Was Eight-Year-Old

- Air Raid 55
- With Mom 59
- Minowa Town 63
- Methamphetamine 65
- Alcoholic 67
- Domestic Violence 71
- Farewell 77
- Masahiro's Heart 79

第五章　沈黙をすて　——一二歳の紘子

　炎のしたで 86
　夜　叉 88
　父の実印 94
　涼子ちゃん！　ごめんね 100
　ありがとう 106
　沈黙をすて 112

第六章　六六年目の　おびえ　——九歳の和子

　六六年目の　おびえ 118
　戦争孤児の思い 120
　小さなお母さん 122
　震災によせ 128
　戦争孤児茉莉 132
　復興と平和を 136

　跋文　弁護士　原田　敬三 140
　あとがき 150
　日英詩集に寄せるご挨拶 156

Chapter 5 Breaking Silence; Hiroko Was Twelve-Year-Old

Under Fire ⋯⋯ 87
Yaksha ⋯⋯ 89
Father's Registered Seal ⋯⋯ 95
I'm So Sorry, Ryoko-Chang! ⋯⋯ 101
Thank You! ⋯⋯ 107
Breaking Silence ⋯⋯ 113

Chapter 6
The Sixty-Sixth Year of Fear; Kazuko Was Nine-Year-Old

The Sixty-Sixth Year of Fear ⋯⋯ 119
Thought of War Orphans ⋯⋯ 121
Little Mother ⋯⋯ 123
For Disaster ⋯⋯ 129
Mari, War Orphan ⋯⋯ 133
For Reconstruction and Peace ⋯⋯ 137

Background Explanation by Keizo Harada (Lawyer) ⋯⋯ 141
Afterwards by Yoko Asami ⋯⋯ 151

Greetings to the revised Japanese & English poetry collection
⋯⋯ 157

第一章　独りぽっちの人生
　　　——六歳の智恵子

Chapter 1
A Sole, Daily Life;
Chieko Was Six-Year-Old

夕　日

――　私は　今でも　夕日が　嫌いです

語気を強め　言い切る　石川智恵子　六九歳
東京大空襲訴訟で　証人尋問にたつ　彼女
打合せ場所を　わが家にした　代理人の夫
二人の　傍らで　茶を入れながら
彼女の話に　聞き入った

三月一日　六歳の誕生日をむかえた　智恵子は
深川で　三月一〇日の　東京大空襲にみまわれ
両親と　二人の兄弟を
亡くしたと言う

あの日　一二歳の姉に　背負われ
智恵子が　目にした　光景とは
焼けて小さくなった　黒い死体が
道いっぱいに　折り重なり
人が歩ける分だけ
脇にどけられていた
まさに　地獄だったと言う

一二歳の長女と一〇歳の長兄
智恵子が　生き残った
翌日　三人は
別々の親戚に　引き取られた

Sunset

—— Even now, still, I'm not too fond of sunset.

She goes on to say in a hushed tone, Chieko Ishikawa, who was a sixty-nine-year-old woman.
She stands in court to question witnesses for the Tokyo Air Raid.
My husband, the attorney, has chosen our house as the meeting place.
I sat beside them, making tea,
And I listened to her story.
She goes on to say in a hushed tone, again and again.

Chieko celebrates her sixth birthday on 1 March, nevertheless,
In Fukagawa, alas, she was hit by the Tokyo Air Raid on March 10th.
At that time, she lost her parents
And two siblings...

On that day, with her twelve years old sister on her back,
Chieko saw a gruesome scene...
The burnt and small black corpse
Folded over and over, filling the road,
Only enough for a person to walk on.
The bodies were moved aside.
She said it was truly hell!

The Eldest daughter aged twelve, the eldest brother aged ten,
And Chieko survived. They are the only survivors in their family.
The next day, they were taken in
By separate relatives.

その日から
智恵子の　孤独との
戦いが　始まった

六歳の智恵子は
労働力には　ならない
役に立たない
彼女の　食事は
小さい芋　一個か
一握りの　ご飯だけ
みそ汁の　味も
お新香の　味も
知らないでいた

家に　居場所を　持てない
智恵子は
夕日に　向かい
お父ちゃん！　お母ちゃん！
一人泣きながら
叫んでいたと言う

土手の夕日が　沈むころ
そっと帰り　部屋の隅に
隠れるように
座っていたと語る

小学校に入った　智恵子に
姉の居場所が　知らされた
学校で必要な　一切を
姉から　貰うためにだ

From that day
Chieko's battle has begun.
Her enemy's name was loneliness.

Six-year-old Chieko is
Not useful in the workforce.
Yes, she's useless.
She eats only
A small potato,
Or a handful of rice,
In addition, she didn't know,
No taste of miso soup,
Or the taste of pickled vegetables.

Chieko has no place at home.
And often she used to shout,
Facing the setting sun,
"Oh, Dad! Ohhhh, Mom!"
Crying, all by herself.
She said that she was shouting.

When the sun sets on the bank,
She said that she used to return home quietly.
And she sat in the corner of the room,
As if she was hiding.

When Chieko entered elementary school,
She was informed of her sister's whereabouts.
Because she had to get everything
She needed it for school from her sister.

小学校を出た　姉は
女中奉公で　給金を貰い
食べることも　できていた

長く延びた　黒い影が
田畑にとけこみ
夕日の落ちた　あぜ道を
智恵子は　姉の所に
行かなくてはと
心細さに　ふるえ
涙をこらえ　一心に
歩いたものだと話した

明るい時間に
姉の所に着くと
家に返されるので
夕日を背に
暗くなってから
辿りつくようにと
子どもなりの
知恵だったと
苦笑した

六三年経った　いまも
夕日は　智恵子を
幼い日の　不安で
寂しかった日々にと
引き戻す

At that time, her sister had already graduated from elementary school,
And she could afford it for her daily life
By working as a living maid.

Long black shadows stretched out.
And blended in with the fields...
Along the path where the sun has set,
Chieko must go to her sister's.
She shivered with anxiety,
And held back her tears.
She told me
How she used to walk along the road.

In the light of day,
When she gets to my sister's,
She would be returned to her house.
So, she devised the way
To arrive at her house,
After dark, with the setting sun in the background.
She remembered it,
And laughed,
It was merely a child's wisdom.

Now, sixty-three years have passed,
The setting sun still haunts Chieko.
Back to the anxious day,
And lonely days,
Of her childhood...

子　守

やせ細り　お腹が膨らんだ
小学校三年生の　智恵子
見かねた　近所の人が
子守の世話を　してくれた

智恵子の背に　伝わる
命の温もり　命の鼓動
彼女の中に　宿った情
乳飲み子への　慈しみ

めざしと　みそ汁
子守先の家で　初めて
家族と同じ　食事をした
彼女は　喜びと安堵のなか

生きねばならないことを
受け入れた

差　別

二四歳　三度の転校後
夜間中学校を卒業
取得した
和文タイプの資格をもち

Babysitting

Chieko was thin, and her stomach was distended.
She was a third grader in elementary school.
Neighbors couldn't bear to overlook her situation.
They gave her the job of babysitting.

The warmth of life and the heartbeat of life,
Could be felt on Chieko's back.
The love that resided within her,
The compassion for a nursing baby.

Dried sardines and miso soup!
For the first time at the house where she was babysitting.
She ate the same meal as her family.
She was filled with joy and relief.

She accepted the fact
That she had to live.

Discrimination

She was twenty-four years old and after three times moving,
Eventually, she graduated from night junior high school.
And she obtained Japanese typing qualifications,
And she tried job hunting,

就職活動を
が　面接で

──　高校も出ていない者に
　　　タイプが　打てるはずがない

と　資格を否定された

智恵子は　迷わず
夜間高校に進んだ
両親や保証人のいない
彼女に
終生つきまとった
差別

　　　　　　　結　婚

三四歳になった　智恵子に
縁談話がきた
二歳になった男の子を残し
妻に先だたれた男(ひと)との
縁談話だった

黄色く　くすんだ顔
手足の垢は
痂(かさぶた)　になっていた
彼女は　この子に

But,
At an interview…

—— Hahaha, you haven't even finished high school!
　　So there is no way you can type!

She was denied her occupational competence.

Chieko did not hesitate
And enrolled in a night high school.
But she has been discriminated against
All her life.
Because she had
No parents or guarantors…

Marriage

At the age of thirty-four,
Chieko got an offer.
It was about a marriage proposal.
The scheduled man was a widower.
He had a two-year-old boy.

The boy's face was yellow and dull.
The grime on his hands and feet were
Crusted over.
She stared at the boy.

幼い日の
自分を　重ね見た

──　私の命を　この子にあげよう

と　この男(こ)を
慈しみ育てようと
母の道を
迷うことなく　選んだ
石川智恵子　三四歳の
人生の　決断

祈　り

出された茶には
手をつけず
淡々と話す　智恵子

彼女は　五三歳の時
蜘蛛膜下出血し
生死を　さ迷ったそうだ

その時の事を
子どもが　話してくれた

──　凄く　怯えていたよ
──　苦しそうに　叫んでいたよ

He was just like when I was a little girl,
She thought.

—— I'll give him my whole life.

She wanted to nurture him
With love and care.
She chose to be a mother.
Without hesitation.
Chieko Ishikawa, who was thirty-four years old.
This was truly the decision of life.

Pray

She didn't touch the tea served.
But she continues taking,
Just plainly.

At the age of fifty-three,
She suffered a subarachnoid hemorrhage.
She wondered between life and death.

Her child told me,
About that time.

—— She was so scared.
—— She was screaming in agony.

――母さんは　大変な苦労を
　　　して来たんだなと　思ったよ

と　嬉しそうに語った
彼女には　今でも
後遺症があるそうだ

六歳で止まった
壊されたままの
心の時計
不安と恐怖と怒り
家族を慕う
狂おしい　孤独

わたしは　涙を押しかくし
新しい茶を　入れかえながら
彼女の心の
癒される日が来ることを
智恵子さんの怒りが
解かれる日を　願った

—— And I thought
    "Mom, you've been through a lot".

Her children recalled the occasion merrily.
It is said that
She's still got the aftereffects.

Her clock of life,
Has stopped since she was six.
Broken and still broken.
Anxiety, fear, and anger.
Longing for her family,
Crazy loneliness.

I couldn't show them my tears.
As I refill the new cup of tea.
I wished for the day when her heart would be healed.
I wished for the day when Chieko's anger,
Would be disappeared,
Too.

第二章　こわれた心
　　　——一歳の幸一

Chapter 2
The Broken Heart;
Koichi Was One-Year-Old

別　れ

一九四五年三月一〇日　未明
風の音と　重なりながら
Ｂ29の飛来音がした
城東区大島の夜空には
真っ赤な炎が　爪を立て
熱風が　渦巻き
燃える　電線が
荒れ狂っていた

母の背に負ぶわれ
命をつないだ
一歳の　幸一
この夜　父は
町内の人の
安否を気遣って
妻子を　逃がし
その場に　止まった
彼は　父の顔も　声も
知ることなく育った

母は　五人の子を
女手一つで育てた
母は　生活保護を
受けながら
父の分まで　働いた

中学を出た兄さん

Separation

It was 10 March 1945, early morning.
Overlapping with the sound of the wind,
Boeing B-29 Superfortress flew overhead.
In the night sky over Oshima in Joto-ku,
Bright red flames clawed their way up.
Hot winds whipped up in a whirlwind,
Burning power lines.
They were raging wildly.

Because he was carried
On his mother's back,
One-year-old Koichi miraculously survived.
But on that night, his father
Concerned for the safety of his neighbors
And he let his wife and child escape.
He dared to stop under the great Tokyo Air Raid.
He grew up
Without knowing
His father's face or voice.

His mother raised five children.
All by herself.
She was on welfare.
His mother worked very hard,
Enough to make up for her husband's absence.

His brother and sister started working,

中学を終えた姉さんも　働いた
極貧生活は　幸一から
笑顔と言葉を　奪っていた
彼は　焼け跡のバラックから
小学校に入学した

彼は　友だちに
心を開くことができなかった
彼は　先生に
心を開くことができないでいた
教室の隅で　黙々と
絵を描きつづける　幸一だった

子犬のシロ

幸一が　三年生になった
学校帰りの　ある雨の日
傘を持たない彼は
強い雨に　打たれ
びしょ濡れになり
うなだれ　歩いていた

キュン　キューンと鳴く
子犬の　か細い声
幸一は　立ち止まり
あたりを　見まわした
煤(すす)け　壊れた

As soon as they graduated from junior high school.
Living in extreme poverty
Koichi was deprived of his smiles and words.
He entered elementary school,
From burnt-out barracks.

He couldn't open up
To his friends.
He couldn't open up
To his teachers, too.
In the corner of the classroom,
Koichi continued drawing pictures.

Shiro, the Puppy

Koichi started third grade.
One rainy day after school,
He didn't even have an umbrella.
By the strong rain, he was drenched.
He got soaked to the skin
And he was walking with a nod.

"Whine, Whine!"
Koichi heard the muffled cries of a puppy.
Then he stopped
And looked around.
Cowering in the corner of a brick wall,

煉瓦塀の隅に　うずくまり
雨に　打ち震える
白い子犬が　そこにいた

彼は　濡れた子犬を
そっと抱き上げ　懐にいれた

幸一は　家族に内緒で
子犬を　飼うことにした
焼けたトタンと
段ボールで作った　犬小屋
彼は　脱脂粉乳を
空き缶に入れ　子犬に飲ませた
学校給食の　パンを
少し残して　持ち帰っていた

幸一は　子犬を
シロと　名付けた
彼は　シロと
無二の親友になった
学校帰り　毎日
シロと　たわむれた

彼は　シロと笑った
シロと　話をしていた
彼は　シロから
生きる喜びを　貰っていた

That was blackened and reduced to rubble.
Shivering in the rain,
A white puppy was there.

He gently picked up this wet puppy
And wrapped it in his clothing.

Koichi decided to keep the puppy,
But he didn't tell his family.
A kennel made of burnt tin and corrugated cardboard.
He filled an empty can with skimmed milk powder
And gave it to the puppy.
He brought home a bit of bread
From the school lunch.

Koichi named the puppy Shiro.
It derives from its white fur.
He and Shiro became
Best friends, indeed.
Every day after school,
He played with Shiro.

He laughed with Shiro.
Talking with Shiro.
From Shiro,
He got his joy of life!

こわれた心

シロと過ごす　楽しい毎日
幸一に　訪れた
つかの間の　安らぎ

そんな　ある日
地下足袋に　ねじり鉢巻きをした
三人の大人が
幸一とシロを　取り囲んだ

――生活保護を　受けてる者(もん)が
　　犬を飼う　なんぞとは

幸一の膝で遊ぶ　シロの後ろ首を
一人の男が無造作に　つかみあげた
キューン　キューンと鳴く　シロの声
助けを求める　シロの　悲しい声を残し
シロは　男たちに　連れ去られてしまった

為す術もなく
拳を握り　涙をこらえ
男たちの後ろ姿を
見つづけた　幸一

あの日　彼のなかに　怒りがわいた
あの時　彼のなかの　心がこわれた

Broken Heart

Happy days with Shiro.
Koichi fully enjoyed,
A momentary peace of mind.

Then one day,
Three adults
In split-toe socks and twisted headbands
Surrounded Koichi and Shiro.

—— What a luxury for a welfare recipient,
　　To have a canine! You are an Idiot!

At that time, Shiro played on Koichi's lap.
A man grabbed the puppy by the back of the neck.
Shiro cries,"Whine,Whine!"
Leaving Shiro's sad voice begging for help,
They took him away.

Koichi, helpless,
Clenched his fists,
Fought back tears.
Stared at the men's backs.

On that day, anger rose in him.
At that time, his heart broke completely...

幸一の戦後

壊れた心を抱え
過ごした　幸一の戦後
一九四五年三月一〇日の夜
家族から　奪われたものが
何だったかを　考えた

彼は　下町の隅で
静かに息を引き取った
母の一生を　思い起こした
五人の子を育てるために
懸命に働いた　母

節くれた手指
深く曲がった腰
老いてなお
働き続けた　母だった

母を支え
幼い弟妹のために
過酷な労働条件で
働きとおした
長兄の　長女の
辛く厳しかった
青春を
思いめぐらした

貧しさ故に

Koichi's Post-War

With a broken heart
Koichi spent the post-war period.
He kept thinking about
What exactly was taken from his family,
On the night of March 10, 1945.

He cared for his mother,
But she passed away in the environs of downtown.
As he did so, he recalled his mother's whole life.
She was a woman who had worked hard, really hard,
To raise her five children.

Her knobby fingers.
Her deeply bent back.
Even in her old age,
She worked and worked and worked…

He thought about,
The difficult and harsh youth,
Of his eldest brother and sister.
They had supported their mother,
And worked hard,
Very hard,
Under difficult conditions
To provide for their younger siblings.

Discrimination and belittlement,

受けた　差別と　さげすみ
貧しさ故に
友をもたず　孤立した日々

安らぎを拒み
壊れた心で　過ごした
幸一の六三年の人生
彼は　彼の人生にいまだ
戦後が　来ていないことを
確信した

二〇〇七年三月九日
東京地方裁判所に
提訴された
東京大空襲訴訟原告団の
一人に　加藤幸一
六三歳の　名があった

三月一〇日の　東京大空襲を　境に
家族が　背負った　苦しい人生の
原因を　はっきりさせたいと
裁判に　立ち上がった

Because of their poverty.
Isolated, friendless, daily life,
Because of his poverty.

Refusing to be at peace,
Spent the rest of his life with a broken heart,
Koichi's sixty-three years of life.
He was convinced that
The post-war period
Had not yet come for him.

On March 9, 2007.
Koichi Kato,
Sixty-three years old man,
Was one of the plaintiffs,
In the Tokyo Air Raid Lawsuit,
Filed in the Tokyo District Court.

He decided to go to court
To clarify the causes of the difficult life
That his family had been forced to live,
After the March 10 air raid on Tokyo…

第三章　うばわれた魂
　　　──三歳の由美子

Chapter 3
The Swallowed Soul;
Yumiko Was Three-Year-Old

叔母の背

叔母の背に　負ぶさった
三歳の　青木由美子
叔母の背の　温もりに
安らぎを
得ていたのだろう

三月一〇日の夜を
とっても　明るい夜
パラパラと　落ちる
火の粉が
とても綺麗だと
思ったと……
由美子に　残された
唯一の　肉親との
温もりの　記憶

一九四五年三月一〇日
叔母に背負われ　紡いだ命
だが　この夜を　さかいに
彼女からは
命と引き替えに
あたり前の　生活が
奪われていた

Aunt's Back

Yumiko Aoki, who was three years old
Was carried on her aunt's back.
She must have found comfort
In the warmth of
Her aunt's back.

Yumiko reminded
The night of March 10th.
It was a very bright night.
Fire sparks,
Flickering...
She thought it was very beautiful.
Yumiko's only memory
Of her immediate family,
Memories of warmth.

On March 10, 1945.
Yumiko's life spun out on her aunt's shoulders.
But from on that night.
In exchange for her life,
The normal daily life
Was taken from her,
Completely.

伯母の家で

　　由美子が　五歳のとき
　　東京の母の実家から
　　父の実家　新潟県糸魚川市に
　　そして
　　父の姉の　嫁ぎ先に　と……

　　――お前のお父さんの学費を
　　　　出したのに
　　　　返しもしないで
　　　　死んでしまうとは
　　　　そして　こんどは　お前かい……

　　臨月間近の　伯母の　怖い視線
　　冷たく　言い放たれた　言葉は
　　幼い　由美子の　心に
　　杭となって　打ちこまれた

　　年の近い　従兄弟たちから離された
　　一人きりの　あらたな　生活
　　階段下の　土間での　寝起き

　　小学校　入学への　不安が
　　幼い由美子に　ストレスを与え
　　下痢となって　彼女を　襲った

　　トイレに間に合わず　そそうをする
　　冬の夜　凍てついた　土の上に立たせ

At Her Aunt's House

When Yumiko was five,
From her mother's family home in Tokyo
To her father's family in Itoigawa City, Niigata Prefecture.
And then to my father's sister's marriage...
She was sent on a bureaucratic runaround to relatives!

—— How shameful
    That we raised money for your father's tuition,
    But he died
    Without paying us back!
    And now we have to take care of you...

Yumiko's aunt, who was in the last month of pregnancy,
Glared at her fiercely, like a stake.
The cruel and unkind words...
They inflicted serious damage on Yumiko's heart.

A new life began for her,
Alone and separated from her cousins of close in age.
She had to sleep and wake up on the dirt floor under the stairs.

Anxiety about entering elementary school
Caused stress in little Yumiko,
Which in turn caused her to have diarrhoea.

Auntie despised Yumiko,
Who could not get to the toilet in time and had to urinate profusely.

伯母は　震える由美子の　下半身に
凍りつく水を　無造作にかけた

お腹が冷え　お腹が痛み
また　そそうをする　繰り返しに
脱水症状を　起こした　由美子だが

――お腹が痛いの　寒いの
　　お水が　飲みたいの

と訴え
助けを求める事はできない

小学校から　高校卒業までの
一二年間を　過ごした
伯母の家での　生活は
彼女から　言葉を　奪い
生きる力を
表情を　奪っていた

恐　怖

学校から　由美子の
高校進学を　勧められた
伯父は　恥をかかされたと
ひどく怒った
いきなり　右腕をつかまれ

She made Yumiko stand on the frozen earth on winter nights
And poured freezing water haphazardly over her shivering lower body.

Her stomach got cold, and her stomach ached.
She got diarrhoea again, and the cycle repeated itself,
Eventually, Yumiko was dehydrated.

—— My stomach hurts. I'm cold.
   I need to drink water.

She tried to say so,
But she couldn't ask for help.

From elementary school to high school graduation.
She spent the first twelve years of her life
At her aunt's house.
She was deprived of language,
And her power of life.
She had robbed her of expression.

Terror

Yumiko's school advised her
To go to high school.
But her uncle felt humiliated.
He was furious.
He suddenly grabbed her right arm.

彼女は　裏のたんぼに
連れ出された

頭を　顔を　なぐられた
身体を蹴られ　突き倒された
立ち上がった　彼女のお腹に
石のような拳が　めり込んだ

伯父からの　激しい暴力
由美子が　この家に来て
はじめて持った　感情
それは　恐怖だった

この夜の　出来事は
皮肉にも　彼女に
自分の意志を
芽生えさせた

高校を　卒業したら
大磯にある
エリザベス　サンダースホーム*
で　働きたい

孤児となった
寂しさ　不安
いじめや虐待の
体験を　活かせる
仕事に就こう　と
彼女に　決意させた

She was taken out to the rice paddies
Behind the school.

Her head and face were smacked.
She was kicked in the body,
And pushed down. She got up.
A fist like a stone of his was driven into her stomach.

Violence from her uncle.
Yumiko's first emotion
Since coming to this house
Was terror.

What happened that night was…
Ironically, it gave her
A will of her own.
Her own will.

After graduating from high school.
In Oiso.
Elizabeth Saunders Home*
She sincerely wished to work there.

She was determined to find a job
Where she could use
The loneliness and anxiety
Of being an orphan
And the experience of being a victim
Of bullying and abuse.

＊エリザベス　サンダースホーム＝神奈川県中郡大磯町の児童養護施設。施設の名前は、ホーム設立後、最初の寄付をしてくれた聖公会のある信者の名前から取られた。

声

北陸本線に　最後の汽車が　通るとき
線路わきに　茫然と立つ　彼女を
月明かりが　包みこんでいた
次の瞬間　彼女の　身体が

……　だめ！　生きて　生きるのよ！

耳元で　叫ばれた　激しい声
我に返った　由美子に
寒さと　震えが　おそった
彼女は　もつれる足で　走った
わななく口　あふれでる涙で
家をめざし　夢中で　走った
だが　不思議に　心は　覚めていた

……　あの声は　母さんの声？

由美子の心に　母の存在が　意識された
母への　愛慕を　心深くに　宿しながら
その後の　長い年月を　耐え忍んだ

*Elizabeth Saunders Home = An orphanage in Oiso-machi, Naka-gun, Kanagawa Prefecture, Japan. This faculty was named after a member of the Anglican Church, who made the first donation after Home was established.

Voice

When the last train passes on the Hokuriku Line
She stood stunned by the side of the track.
The moonlight enveloped her.
The next moment, her body...

...... No! Live! You must live!

A fierce voice screamed in her ear.
Yumiko came to herself.
Cold and shivering stunned her.
She ran on faltering legs.
Her mouth gurgled with tears.
She ran like mad for home.
But strangely enough, her mind was still awake.

......Was that Mom's voice?

Yumiko's mind became aware of her mother's presence.
With her love for her mother deep within her,
She endured the long years that followed.

結婚し　二児の母となった　彼女が
母を探そうと　思い立ったとき
五四歳の　由美子の　髪には
すでに　白いものが　まじっていた

二行の命

吉田由美子　五四歳
彼女は　夫とともに
母の所在を　探し訪ねた

やっと手にした　戸籍謄本
由美子には　妹がいた
名前は　恵津子

母穂(イサヲ)の字から　取って
名付けられたのだろうと
由美子には　そう思えた

昭和一九年一一月二五日生
昭和二〇年三月一〇日死亡

戸籍謄本に　残された
二行が　妹　恵津子の
命の証を　伝えていた

She married and became the mother of two children.
When she decided to look for her mother...
Fifty-four-year-old Yumiko's hair
Was already stained with white.

Two Lines of Life

Yumiko Yoshida, aged fifty-four.
She and her husband
Went looking for her mother's whereabouts.

They finally got hold of a copy of her family register.
Yumiko had a younger sister.
Her name was Etsuko.

She must have been named
After her mother, Isawo.
That's what it seemed to Yumiko.

Born on November 25, 1944.
Died on March 10, 1945.

Only two lines left
On the family register,
Told younger sister, Etsuko's whole life.

──　わずか　三ヶ月……
　　　　謄本を見なかったら……

叔母の背で見た
明るい夜に　父と母が
わずか　三ヶ月の
妹恵津子の命が
奪われたことを思い知った

二〇〇七年三月九日
数え切れない　苦しみ
哀しみ　寂しさ　不安
不条理を　乗り越え
東京大空襲訴訟原告団の
一人となった　由美子

焼け死んだ　溺れ死んだ魂
凍死した　窒息死した魂
あの夜　奪われた
多くの魂を　胸に

この夜の　出来事を
忘れてはいけない
この夜の　出来事を
伝えなければいけない

この夜　奪われていった
死者たちの　名を刻み
弔いつづけねば　と
彼女は　裁判にのぞんだ

—— She lived only three months...
   If Yumiko hadn't seen register...

Yumiko finally understood.
On the bright night that her aunt carried Yumiko on her back,
She learned the fact not only her father and mother,
But also her three-month-old sister Etsuko's life
Had been lost.

On March 9, 2007.
Overcoming countless suffering,
Sorrow, loneliness, anxiety,
And absurdity,
Yumiko became one of the plaintiffs
In the Tokyo Air Raid Lawsuit.

Burnt to death, drowned souls.
The souls that froze to death, the souls that suffocated.
Deprived of souls that night.
Many souls in her heart.

What happened that night...
She determined, that she must not forget.
She must tell the story of what happened that night.
She has to tell the people, all over the world.

She thought she must remember
The names of the dead.
And she tried to continue to mourn them.
So, she went to trial.

第四章　三ノ輪の町で
　　——八歳のマサヒロ

Chapter 4
At Minowa Town;
Masahiro Was Eight-Year-Old

空襲

一九四五年三月一〇日　未明
江東　墨田　台東　と
下町住民を
猛火に　閉じ込め
東京の三分の一を　焼いた
東京大空襲

小学校一年生の　マサヒロは
家族とともに
三ノ輪の町で
東京大空襲に　みまわれた

「今夜は　ひどいのが来るぞ！
　防空壕なんかじゃ
　やられちまうぞ！」
九日　旋盤工の　父は
仕事あがりに　言った

たえまなく鳴る
空襲警報の　サイレン
サーチライトが　夜空を
縦横に　てらす
B29の　大きな　機体が
つぎからつぎへと　とんでくる

シュルシュル
シュルシュル

Air Raid

At dawn, 10 March 1945.
Koto, Sumida, Taito and
Downtown residents
Were trapped in a raging fire.
One third of Tokyo was burnt to the ground.
Tokyo Air Raid.

Masahiro was a first grader of elementary school.
With his family
In the town of Minowa,
He had suffered the Tokyo Air Raid.

"There's going to be a terrible one tonight !
　We can't stay in the air raid shelter.
　We'll get hit!"
On the ninth, his father, a lathe operator.
Said to his family after work.

The air raid sirens were
Going off incessantly.
The searchlights illuminated
The night sky in all directions.
The big B-29 Superfortress flew
One after another.

Shrrrrrrrrrrrr!
Shrrrrrrrrrrrrr!

焼夷爆弾が
雨のように
降り落ちるなか
ドカーン
ズズズーン
爆弾が　落ちるなか

母は　二歳になった
次男を　おぶい
五歳の　三女の手を
右手に握り　左手には
国民学校一年生の
長男マサヒロの手を　ひいて

家が　人が　燃えるなか
炎と熱風に　追われながら
人波におされ
逃げまわり　走りまわった

一〇日未明の
風速三〇メートル近い
強風が　炎と熱風を
狂気に　かりたてていた

おひつを抱え　飛び出した
長女の　姿が　ない
みんなを　守っていてくれた
父の　姿が　ない
舅(しゅうと)さんは　と
立ちすくんだ　しゅんかん

Incendiary bombs
Falling down like rain
Boooooooom!
Zoom! Zoom!
As the bombs fell...

His mother was carried
Her second son, two-year-old.
She also held the hand of her third daughter, aged five,
In her right hand and in left hand,
She held the hand of her eldest son,
Masahiro, a first grade of national school...

While houses and people were burning
Chased by flames and hot winds
He was swept away by the waves of people.
They fled, and ran and ran.

In the early hours of the morning of the 10th
The winds were blowing at nearly 30 meters per hour,
And the flames and the heat
Glew harshly.

The eldest daughter was nowhere to be found.
She ran out of the house, carrying Ohitsu.
Her father was nowhere to be found.
The man who protected us all...
Then, where's father-in-law?
She stood still.

「おトリ　いいか！
　　焼け跡に　にげろ！」
たしかに
母の名を　呼ぶ
父の　声がした

母ちゃんと

母は　幼子二人の　手を
もう一度　強く握りしめた

「いいかい　マサヒロ
　ユキオを　見てとくれ！
　やけどをしないように
　火の粉が　飛んできたら
　母ちゃんに　教えとくれ！
　いいかい！」

「わかった　母ちゃん！」

「ヨシコ　なくな！
　ユキオを　見てろ！
　兄ちゃんが　おまえを
　守ってやるから！
　火の粉が　飛んできたら
　兄ちゃんに言え！」

"Otori, listen to me!
  Get away to the burnt ruins!"
Indeed,
He heard his father's voice
Calling Masahiro's mother's name.

With Mom

Mother took the hands of both her toddlers in hers.
Once more she held them tightly.

"Listen, Masahiro.
  Watch over Yukio!
  Don't let him get burned.
  If there are any fire sparks,
  Tell me. I'm your mother.
  Are you okay?"

"Okay, Mom!"

"Yoshiko, stay away!
  Watch over Yukio!
  Your brother will protect you!
  If there are any fire sparks,
  Tell your brother,
  Are you Okay?"

「わかったよ！　母ちゃん！」

母ちゃんと　いっしょに
弟と妹を　守るんだと
マサヒロは　母ちゃんの手を
ぎゅっと　握りかえした

常磐線と　汐留の引き込み線の
まくら木が　燃え
親子ガードは　大きな火の手を
あげていた
土手に　あがった　人たちを
火の粉が　おそう
衣服についた　火が
人を　焼く

二月二五日の　空襲で
常磐線の　反対側
南千住二丁目　一帯は
焼け野原と　なっていた
親子ガードを　ぬければ
二丁目の　焼け跡が……

たしかに　聞こえた
父の声を　たよりに
母と　泣くことを忘れた
子どもたち　三人

まくら木が　人が　燃えるなか
ガード下を

"Okay, Mom!"

Determined to protect his brother and sister
Together with his mother,
Masahiro squeezed her hand back
Tightly.

The sleeper barriers of the Joban Line
And the Shiodome Line caught fire.
Oyako guarder bridge
Was on big fire.
The fire sparks were pouring down on
The people who were on the bank.
Fire on clothes
Burned people.

On the 25th of February, in the Air Raid.
On the other side of the Joban Line,
Minami Senju 2-chome,
Was burnt to the ground.
If they went through Oyako guarder bridge
They could have seen the burnt ruins of 2-chome....

The mother and the three children,
Who had forgotten how to cry, ran.
They ran towards their father's voice,
Which they believed they had heard.

While sleepers and people were burning,
They ran with all their might

焼け跡　めざし
いっしんふらんに　走りきった

三ノ輪の町

マサヒロが　通った
第二瑞光小学校の　青柳は
真っ黒にこげ　炭になって
校庭に　立っていた

マサヒロが　育った
三ノ輪の町は　あたり一面
黒く焼けこげた　がれきの
死人の　山になっていた

マサヒロが　遊んだ
路地裏や　表通りは
こげた臭いが　鼻をつき
目がしみ　喉が痛かった

気がつくと
三ノ輪の町が
黒く炭に　なっていた

Toward the burnt ruins
Beyond the under the guarder bridge.

Minowa Town

Masahiro went to.
Aoyagi at the Second Zuiko Elementary School.
'Blackened and burned to charcoal,
They were standing in the schoolyard.

Where Masahiro grew up.
The town of Minowa was burnt to a crisp.
Blackened and burnt to a crisp.
It was a pile of dead people.

Masahiro went to the back alleys and front streets where he used to play,
But the burnt smell was coming up his nose,
His eyes were blotchy
And his throat was sore.

Now he understood the fact that
The town of Minowa
Blackened to charcoal.

ヒロポン

一七歳のマサヒロ兄さんは
学校を休み
四・五人の仲間と　家で遊んでいた
ドラムの練習だと　ところ構わず
バチをたたき　リズムをきざんだ

麻疹で熱を出し　母に抱かれ
苦しむ　四歳の妹の姿など
彼の目には　届かなかった
彼らは　ドラムの練習に
興じていた

一七歳のマサヒロ兄さんは
学校を休む
ポマードで　両脇を固め
前髪を　深く垂らし
リーゼントにした頭で
肩で　風きり
浅草ロック街を
意気込んで　歩いた

そんな　ある日
昼間なのに
兄さんの　大いびきが
障子をそっと開け
部屋を　覗いた
注射器と

Methamphetamine

Brother Masahiro, a 17-year-old young man,
Had skipped school
And was playing at home with four or five friends.
They were practicing their drumming skills.
They beat the sticks and played the rhythm.

He ignored his four-year-old sister,
Who was suffering from a fever caused by measles
And was being nursed by her mother.
The delinquent boys were busy practicing their drumming.

Brother Masahiro, a 17-year-old young man,
Skipped school, again.
His fringes, held in place on both sides by pomades,
Hung down deeply
And his hairstyle was in a regent.
He walked with gusto down
On Asakusa Rokkugai,
Wind whipping at his shoulders.

Then one day
In the daytime...
Brother Masahiro snoring loudly.
His mother gently opened the shoji screen.
She peeked into his room.
A syringe

薄茶色のゴムひもが
マサヒロ兄さんのそばに
無造作に
放り出されていた

ヒロポンを買う　お金をせびり
母を泣かせた　マサヒロ兄さん
町で　不良仲間と喧嘩しては
警察に　何度も　補導された
マサヒロ兄さんは
練馬の少年鑑別所にも送られた

アルコール依存症

ヒロポンを止めさせようと
父が教えた　お酒
マサヒロ兄さんは
浴びるように　酒を呑んだ
そして　心を壊し
身体をこわした

酒代を作るために　兄さんは
焼け残った　母の着物を
背広を　姉のコートを
こうもり傘を　質に入れた
手当たりしだい　質に入れ
酒を呑んだ

And a light brown rubber band
Placed by brother Masahiro's side.
Carelessly
They were thrown out in the open.

He asked her for money to buy Methamphetamine.
He made my mother cry.
He got into fights with other delinquents in town.
He was repeatedly taken into custody by the police.
Eventually brother Masahiro
Was even sent to the Nerima Juvenile Detention Center.

Alcoholic

Tried to get him to stop using Methamphetamine.
His father taught him to drink alcohol.
Young Masahiro drank as much as he could.
He drank like a fish.
And he broke down.
He got sick.

To pay for it,
He took my mother's clothes that were left over from the fire.
My mother's kimono, my suit, my sister's coat...
He pawned his sister's coat and his umbrella.
He pawned whatever he could get his hands on.
Brother Masahiro,

マサヒロ兄さん

友達に　お金を借りて
酒を呑んだ
近所の　酒屋さんで
後で払うから　と言って
酒を呑んだ
銀座や　浅草の
バーや　キャバレーで
月末払いだ　と言って
付けで　酒を振る舞い
酒を呑んだ

弟の修学旅行の積立金で
月謝で　酒を呑んだ
マサヒロ兄さんの酒代で
家族の生活は　極貧に
家族の心は　切り裂かれた

——　お前に　これ以上
　　　酒を呑ます　金などない

突っぱねた　父

薄ら笑いをした兄は
ツバを吐きながら　階段をおり
台所の床板に　米櫃(こめびつ)に　障子に
ガソリンを　ふりかけ
ぷいっと　家を出て行った

He drank like a fish.

He borrowed money from friends
And drank.
He went to a liquor shop in the neighborhood.
He said he'd pay later.
At bars and cabarets in Ginza and Asakusa
He served them drinks
And he told them
That he would pay at the end of the month.
He drank like a fish.

With the money from his brother's school excursion fund.
With the money from the monthly fees.
Masahiro's drank like a fish.
The family lived in extreme poverty.
The family's heart was torn asunder.

——— We have no money to give you any more.
    Stop drinking alcohol!

His father refused.

Masahiro, with a wry smile,
Spitting and down the stairs.
He poured petrol on the kitchen floorboards,
The rice bin, the shoji screens.
He left the house in a hurry.

米を買い換える　お金はない
家族は　ガソリン臭い　ご飯を
もくもくと　食べつづけた
母に　姉や弟妹に向ける
兄の　怒りと　いやがらせ

父は　そんな　兄を
突き放そうとはしなかった
……　……

家庭内暴力

お金がたりないと　夜中に
お金をせびりに　帰ってきた
マサヒロ兄さん
お金は無い　と言うと
暴れて　母を　なじった

──　そんなに　あたしが
　　　憎いなら　殺しとくれ！

母は押し入れの前に座り合掌した
泣きながら　母に抱きついた私
二人の肩越しに　兄がなげた
アイロンが　飛んできた
押し入れの板戸が　破れた

The family has no money to buy new rice.
The family kept eating rice
That smelled of petrol.
Masahiro's angry and harassing.
Against his mother. his sisters and brothers.

But his father,
Never abandoned Masahiro
......

Domestic Violence

Brother Masahiro came home in the middle of the night
Bumming for money.
Her mother told him,
She didn't have any money.
He went on a rampage, taunting his mother.

—— If you hate me so much...
    Kill me!

She sat down in front of the closet and held her hands together.
I hugged her, sobbing.
Over our shoulders, my brother threw
An iron at us.
The wardrobe door was ripped open.

マサヒロ兄さんが二三歳のとき
父は喉頭癌で　死んだ
母と　六人の子を残し
だが　兄の暴力に
終わりなどない

怯える母へのなじりは
姉弟にと　向けられた
一八歳の弟を　布団から引き出し
取っ組み合いをはじめた
二階の手すりに覆い被さる二人
兄は　小さい兄さんの首を
本気で締めていた
小さい兄さんの顔が　真っ青だ
このままでは……　とっさに
こたつの台を　兄さんに
振り上げた　一二歳のわたし

―― 貴様ら　みんなバカだ！
　　見てろ　ほえ面かくな！

そう言い放ち　出て行った

ある夜　いつものように
酔っぱらって帰ってきた
マサヒロ兄さん
ライトバンに　乗って
何処かに　出かけようとした

事故でも起こされては　大変だ

When brother Masahiro was twenty-three.
His father died of laryngeal cancer.
He left his wife and six children.
But my brother's violence…
There was no end in sight.

His taunts were directed at his frightened mother
And it turned his wrath on his siblings
He pulled her eighteen-year-old brother out of the bedclothes.
They started fighting.
They covered each other on the upstairs balustrade.
He was really tightening his little brother's neck.
The little brother's face turned blue.
If things continue like this…
Immediately, I swung the heated table stand at him.
I was twelve years old.

—— You're all idiots!
   I'll never forget this humiliation!

He said to us and left.

One night,
As usual, brother Masahiro
Came home drunk.
He got into his light van.
He was going somewhere.

He'd better not get into an accident.

わたしは　兄の後ろ背に抱きつき
懸命に止めた　だが……

運転席に座り　車を動かした兄
わたしは　両手をひろげ
兄の運転を　阻止しようとした
兄は　私がよけることを見越して
車を　動かした

死ぬなら　死んでもいい
目を瞑り　両手を広げた
わたしの手前　一〇センチで
車は　止まった

　──ヨウコ　お前には負けた
　　　お前には　欲がない
　　　他の姉弟たちとは　違うな！

車をおり　何処かに行った
マサヒロ兄さん

肩を落とし　よろけ歩く
兄の後ろ姿の　寂しさが
なぜか　わたしの心を
さわがせた……

I hugged him on the back.
I tried to stop him, but ......

He sat in the driver's seat and started the car.
I opened my arms.
I tried to stop him from driving.
He anticipated that I would swerve.
He moved the car.

I don't care if I die!
I closed my eyes and opened my arms.
He stopped the car
Ten centimeters in front of me.

—— Yoko, you've won.
    You have no cunning.
    You're not like the other siblings!

Brother Masahiro got out the car,
And went away.

I see him staggering about,
His shoulders slumped.
For some reason,
I was so upset...

別れに

わたしの高校生活は　母と一緒
兄さんを　警察にもらい下げに
わたしの大学生活は　母と一緒
兄さんの　精神病院の入退院手続きに

わたしの社会人生活は　兄さんの看病
酒で壊れた兄さんの身体は　ボロボロ
吐血して　近くの　同善病院に　入院
肝硬変で東京医科歯科大学病院に入院

看病生活のなか　マサヒロ兄さんは

——お前には　世話になったな
　　お前に　青い服を着せてやりたい
　　おれが　お前に選んでやるぞ！

——お前が　おれと　もっと
　　年が近かったら　おれの
　　人生も　少し違っていたかもな

——言い訳は　いけないよな！
　　ヨウコ　お前には
　　幸せになって　貰いたかった

——ヨウコ　いまからでも遅くない

Farewell

My high school years were spent with my mother
Going to the police to get my brother.
My college years were spent with my mother
Going through the procedures for my brother's admission and discharge from a mental hospital.

My working life was spent nursing my brother.
His body was in shambles, broken by alcohol.
He was hospitalized at the nearby Dozen Hospital after vomiting blood.
There he was found to have cirrhosis of the liver and was transferred to Tokyo Medical and Dental University Hospital.

While I was nursing him, Brother Masahiro said,

―― I owe you a lot, don't I?
　　I want to dress you in blue.
　　I'll choose the special for you!

―― If you were closer to me
　　In the age,
　　My life would be a little different.

―― No excuses, right?
　　You know, Yoko,
　　I wanted you to be happy, heartily.

―― It's not too late for that, Yoko.

良い人がいたら　結婚しろよ
お前なら　幸せになれるよ！

三〇年前の　マサヒロ兄さんの声が
いまも　わたしの耳に……

マサヒロの心は

マサヒロ兄さんの半生は
酒に逃げ　酒におぼれた

マサヒロ兄さんは人生の大半を
孤独にさいなまれ　じれていた

家族との絆を　修復できぬままに
彼は　昭和五六年一二月
四六歳の　生涯を閉じた

あの夜の惨事　東京大空襲は
少年マサヒロの　心に　どう
関わったのだろうかと……

母と力を合わせ　懸命に
幼い弟と妹の　命を守った
あの夜　マサヒロは
生きることに　全身全霊で
立ち向かっていた

If you find the right man, marry him.
Because you're not cunning, you'll be happy!

I still hear the voice of my brother Masahiro
From thirty years ago...

Masahiro's Heart

Brother Masahiro's life was empty.
He ran away and drowned himself in drinking.

For most of his life.
He was lonely and frustrated.

Unable to mend his family ties.
He passed away in December 1981.
At the age of forty-six.

I wonder what the Tokyo Air Raid
Had to do with the boy Masahiro's mind...
That night was terrible.

He worked hard with his mother
To save the lives of his younger brother and sister.
That night, Masahiro was facing life
With all his might.
He was not a child, but an adult.

彼は　一人の大人だった

彼が　母によせた　労り
弟に妹によせた　慈しみ
あの夜　マサヒロの心は
母や弟妹と　一つとなって
地獄から　生きのびたのだと
家族との一体感を　確信した

あの夜の確信は　その後の
彼の人生を　つらぬき
家族との　深い絆となって
彼を支え　彼を生きさせるはず
だが　思いは　独りよがり……

八歳の　マサヒロは
生きるエネルギーの大半を
燃やし尽くしてしまったが……

幼すぎた弟　恐怖に怯えた妹は
あの夜の　惨事の記憶を遠のけ
兄マサヒロとの　絆はない

終戦後の　貧しさと混乱のなか
母は　あの夜の地獄を封じて生き
マサヒロへの労りも　絆もない

八歳のマサヒロが　命がけで
守った　母と弟妹の命なのに

The care he showed his mother.
The love he showed his brother and sister.
That night, Masahiro's heart
Was one with his mother and siblings.
He had survived the hell he had been through.
He was convinced that he was one with his family.

The conviction of that night
Would carry him through the rest of his life,
Would become the deepest bond he ever had with his family,
Would sustain him and keep him alive,
But he was alone in his thoughts…

Eight-year-old Masahiro.
He has burned up
Most of his energy for life…

His little brother was too young,
His sister was frightened.
They put the memory of that night's tragedy behind them,
No bond with her brother Masahiro.

After the war, in poverty and chaos.
My mother lived her life with the hell of that night sealed away.
There was no care for Masahiro, no bond with him.

Eight-year-old Masahiro risked his life
To protect his mother and siblings.

彼の心は　置き去りにされた

母も　弟妹も　兄の心を
知ろうとはしない　ただ
彼を疎んじ　生きていた

His heart was left behind.

Neither mother nor younger siblings tried to know his heart
They just lived their lives
Without him.

第五章　沈黙をすて
　　　──一二歳の紘子

Chapter 5
Breaking Silence;
Hiroko Was Twelve-Year-Old

炎のしたで

本所区東駒形の　家の二階で
父と並んで寝ていた　紘子は
突然　父にたたき起こされた

異様な空気　目をこすり窓を見た
窓は　真っ赤に染まっていた
Ｂ29から　投下された焼夷爆弾で
外は　火の海となっていたのだ

慌てて階段をおり
母に言われていたように
生後四ヶ月の茂雄を負ぶい
小さな風呂敷き包みを持って
外に　飛び出した
三歳の涼子を負ぶった
母と二人　手を握り
錦糸町の祖父母の家を目指した

燃える炎が　夜空をおおう
熱風で　息が苦しい
そんな中　母と紘子は
人波に　押し潰されないよう
はぐれないよう　声を掛け
人波の中に　身をしずめた

火に囲まれ　人に押され
自分たちの意志では

Under Fire

On the second floor of a house in Higashi Komagata, Honjo Ward
Hiroko was sleeping alongside her father,
But she was suddenly awoken by him.

The strange atmosphere made her rub her eyes
And look at the windows, which were stained red.
Incendiary bombs dropped from B-29 Superfortress
Had turned outside into a sea of fire.

She rushed downstairs,
Carried the four-month-old Shigeo
As her mother had told her,
And took a small furoshiki wrapper with her.
She ran outside.
I carried three-year-old Ryoko on my back.
Her mother and she held hands.
And headed for hr grandparents' house in Kinshicho.

Burning flames covered the night sky.
The hot wind made it hard to breathe.
In the midst of all this, Hiroko and her mother
Called out to each other so that they wouldn't get separated.
Not to get swamped by the crowds,
But they hid themselves in the crowd.

Surrounded by fire, pushed by people.
By our own will.

どこにも　行きようがない

錦糸町への道も　塞がれていた
どこに行くのか　分からぬままに
息苦しいことも　怖さもわすれ
母と紘子は　夢中で逃げ走った

弟を守ろうと　妹を守ろうと
炎のしたを　煙の中を
必死で　走った
母と紘子は　偶然にも
小学校の防空壕に　行きついた

　　＊本所区＝かつての東京府東京市にあり、現・墨田
　　　区の南部。

夜　叉

扉のない防空壕に入ったが
すでに　大勢の人たちが
荷物を残して　壕から
逃げ出し始めていた
逆流する　人波に
逆らうようにして
紘子たちは　壕に入った

壕に残った　親子四人

We couldn't go anywhere by our own will.

The road to Kinshicho was blocked.
We had no idea where we were going.
We forgot about the suffocation and the fear.
Mother and Hiroko ran head over heels.

To protect her brother and sister.
Through fire and smoke.
They ran desperately.
Hiroko and her mother happened to be
In the air raid shelter at the elementary school.

> *Honjo Ward = Formerly part of Tokyo City, Tokyo Prefecture, in the southern part of present-day Sumida Ward.

Yaksha

Hiroko and others I went into
A bomb shelter without a door.
But many people had already left
From the shelter,
Leaving their belongings behind.
Against the surging tide of people,
Hiroko and others entered the shelter.

The Mother and three children remained in the shelter.

紘子は　茂雄を負ぶい
壕の奥に　息をひそめた
紘子は　熱さで
髪が　焼けるかと思った
壕の入り口から　灼熱の空気と
蛇の舌のような炎が　おそう
紘子たちを　呑みこもうと
壕に入ろうと　もがいていた

その時　母は
壕の左すみに　転がっていた
残された二つの位牌を　目にした
涼子を負ぶい　這うようにして
位牌を取りに行った　母

わが子を　守らなければと
人が残して行った　位牌
他人さまの　ご先祖の
慈悲にすがった　母

二つの　お位牌を
壕の入り口に　並べ

　──　南無妙法蓮華経　南無妙法蓮華経
　　　　南無妙法蓮華経　南無妙法蓮華経

飛び込んでくる　火の粉を払い
一心腐乱に　お題目を唱え続けた

　──　南無妙法蓮華経　南無妙法蓮華経

Hiroko was carrying Shigeo.
Deep in the shelter, she hides her breath.
Hiroko was so hot.
She thought her hair would burn.
From the entrance of the shelter
Came the searing air and the flames like a snake's tongue.
They tried to eat Hiroko and the others,
They struggled to get into the shelter.

At that moment, her mother saw
Two mortuary tablets
left in the left-hand corner of the air-raid shelter.
Carrying Ryoko on her back,
Her mother crawled to retrieve the tablets.

Clinging to the tablets left behind by others
And relying on the mercy of other people's ancestors,
Her mother prayed desperately
That she must protect her child.

She placed two tablets
At the entrance of the shelter.

—— Nam-Myoho-Renge-Kyo, Nam-Myoho-Renge-Kyo.
Nam-Myoho-Renge-Kyo, Nam-Myoho-Renge-Kyo.

She brushed off the sparks of fire that flew in.
She repeated the holy chant of Buddhism with all her heart and soul.

—— Nam-Myoho-Renge-Kyo, Nam-Myoho-Renge-Kyo.

　　　　南無妙法蓮華経　南無妙法蓮華経

母の後ろ姿は　真黒な影だった
大きな黒い影が　激しくゆらぎ
火の粉と煙と　赤い炎と格闘し
入口を必死に　守っていた

　――あのとき　母には　何かが
　　のり移っていたのかもしれない

火が鎮火し　壕から出たとき
母の目は　開かなかった

灰にまみれた
黒い母の右手に
絋子は　手を添え
一面が黒くなった
焼け野原の　町を
灰色のうす煙の
立ち残る　町を
我が家を　目指し
恐る恐る　歩き出した

左にのびる細い路地
曲がり角に来たとき
母は立ち止まり　言った

　――この奥に　お寺さんがあるだろう

と　絋子は

Nam-Myoho-Renge-Kyo, Nam-Myoho-Renge-Kyo.

Her mother's back was a pitch-black shadow.
A great black shadow, flickering violently.
She struggled against the sparks of fire, smoke and red flames.
She was desperately protecting the entrance.

—— At that time, something may have
 Haunted her mother...

When the fire was extinguished, they could get out of the bunker
But she couldn't open her eyes.

Hiroko put her hand
On her mother's right hand,
Which was black with ashes.
They set out for their home
In the burnt-out town,
Which had turned black
All over,
She walked fearfully
Through the grey haze of smoke.

A narrow alleyway to the left.
When they came to a turn.
Her mother stopped and said,

—— There's a temple at the end of this road, isn't there?

In response, Hiroko nodded

うん！　とだけうなずき
はやく家にかえろうと
母の手をひっぱり
母を　うながした

東京大空襲訴訟に加わるため
取りよせた　戸籍謄本で
父が　源光寺で
焼死したことを知った

あの日
目の見えなかった
母が　立ち止まり
指差した　お寺だった

父の実印

母が　老人ホームに
入所する　前の日
母は　紘子の前に
古びた印鑑を出した
三月一〇日　空襲の夜
父から　渡されたものだと

あの夜
日頃　穏やかな父が

And said "Yes".
Then she pulled on her mother's hand,
Urging her to keep walking,
To get back home quickly.

To join the Tokyo Air Raid lawsuit.
She got a copy of the family register.
She found out that her father
Was burnt to death at Genkoji Temple.

Genkoji was the temple
Where her mother,
Who was blind that day,
Stopped walking and pointed to!

Father's Registered Seal

The day before my mother was admitted to the nursing home.
She handed Hiroko the old personal seal.
She said it was given to her
By her father.
On March 10,
The night of the Tokyo Air Raid.

That night.
Her father, who was usually so peaceful...

――　子どもたちを連れて
　　　逃げてくれ！

――　お母ちゃんの手を
　　　離すんじゃないぞ！

いつもと違い
大きな　声で
母と　紘子に
どなるように言った

母は　紘子の手を握り
走り出した
父は　走り出した
母を　呼び止め
母の手に印鑑を
確りと　握らせた

この夜　父は
自らの死を
予感したのだろうか

幼いわが子の　今後を案じ
自分の実印と通帳を
母に　託したのだ

この時　母は
父の思いを
悟ったのだろうか

—— Ran away, immediately,
　　Took the children with you!

—— Take your mother's hand!
　　Don't let go!

Like unusual,
Loudly,
He yelled at
His wife and Hiroko.

She grabbed Hiroko's hand.
She started to run.
Her father started to run.
He stops her.
He put the seal in her hand.
He made sure she had a firm grip on it.

That night, he might
Foresee his own death,
Didn't he?

He was worried about the future of his little children
He entrusted his registered seal
And bank book to his wife.

At this time, his wife might
realize her husband's feelings,
Didn't she?

父に託された実印を
父と思い　形見として
今日まで　肌身離さず
持っていたのだそうだ

母は　大切な　父の実印を
自分の実印としていたのだ
そして　いま　その印鑑を
両親二人の　形見とばかり
紘子に　託そうと
母は　取りだした

紘子は　今日まで
何も知らずにいた
母の父を思う　強さと
母と父の　絆の確かさを
いま　知らされた

母は　弱音をはかない人だった
母は　人を責めない人だった
母には　父が寄り添っていたから
母には　寂しさはなかったのだろうと
紘子は　そう思った

She thought that the seal entrusted
From her husband was his very own,
And kept it with her
As a memento of his life to this day.

She had taken her seal as her own.
She used it as her personal seal.
And now she has taken out the seal.
She wanted to leave it
To Hiroko,
As a memento of her parents.

Hiroko had never known
Anything about it until today.
The strength of her mother's love for her father.
And the strength of the bond between mother and father.
Now she knew them.

Her mother was never a complainer.
She never blamed anyone.
Her father was there for his wife.
She was never lonely.
That's what Hiroko thought.

涼子ちゃん！　ごめんね

―― ちゃあちゃん　ぽんぽ　痛いよ！

三歳だった　涼子ちゃんが
この世に　残した　最後のことば
六六年経った　いまも
絋子の耳に　焼きついて　放れない

―― 涼子ちゃん　ごめんね！

三月一〇日の　東京大空襲をのがれ
一二歳の絋子は　母と妹の涼子と
生後四ヶ月の弟茂雄と　ともに
千葉の寒川に　疎開した
母の弟が　兵隊に行っていて
空き家になっている　弟の家に

七月七日　この地で
またしても　機銃掃射の
いっせい攻撃を　受けた
母は　涼子を背負い
絋子が　茂雄を背負った
海岸線を　人波にもまれ
ひた走りに　走った

絋子の　右の手の平に
痛みが　はしった
絋子の手から　ダラダラと

I'm So Sorry, Ryoko-Chang!

—— My tummy hurts, Chaa-Chang (mommie) !

It was the last phrase Ryoko left to this world.
Then, Ryoko was three years old.
Even now, sixty-six years later.
She cannot forget those intense memories.

——I'm So Sorry, Ryoko-Chang!

After surviving the air raid on Tokyo on 10 March,
Twelve-year-old Hiroko evacuated to Samukawa, Chiba,
With her mother, sister Ryoko and four-month-old brother Shigeo.
They were allowed to live in her mother's brother's house,
Which was vacant because he was in the army.

On 7 July, here,
They were again subjected
To the sweep of machine-gun attacks.
Mother carried Ryoko on her back,
And Hiroko carried Shigeo.
They ran along the coastline
Through the crowds.

Pain flared in Hiroko's right palm.
Blood trickled down
From Hiroko's hand.

血が　流れ落ちた
この時
紘子に背負われた　茂雄も
頭に　機銃掃射の
直撃を　受けていた

頭も顔も分からない　ザクロのようだった
茂雄は　泣く声を　上げることなく
四ヶ月という　短すぎる命を　うばわれた

――茂雄ちゃん　ごめんね！

母は　茂雄を　ねんねこ袢纏(はんてん)に包み
人に　踏まれないよう　周りを囲み
海岸の砂に置き　私の手を握り直し
恐怖のなか　またも　逃げまどった

――お母ちゃん　家に帰って
　　みんなで　一緒に　死のうよ

走れども　走れども　追いかけてくる
機銃掃射　逃げ場のない　海岸線
生きようとする　気力の失せた
紘子は　母に言った

この時　母は
何かを　感じたのだろう
自分の腰に　手を回した
その　母の手に　血糊が
ベットリ　はり付いていた

At this time, Shigeo,
Who was being carried on her back,
Also took a direct machine-gun hit
To his head.

Shigeo's head was ruptured,
His head and face were indistinguishable, like a pomegranate.
Shigeo was given four months of his all-too-short life without a cry.

—— I'm So Sorry, Shigeo-Chang!

My mother wrapped Shigeo's body in a babysitting half coat,
Surrounded it to prevent people from stepping on it,
And placed it on the sand on the beach.
Then she reassumed her grip on my hand and ran away again in terror.

——Mom, let's go home together.
    I don't want to die while we remain apart.

No matter how fast they run,
The machine-gun fire will chase them.
They are trapped on the shoreline, with nowhere to run.
Hiroko, who had lost the will to live, told her mother

At this point, her mother,
Perhaps sensing something,
Put her hands around her waist.
Her hands were covered with blood glue.
Ryoko, on her mother's back,

母の背の　涼子も　また
機銃掃射に　やられていた
このままではと……
母も　家に帰ることを決意した

家に着くなり　涼子を寝かせ
きびすを返し　家を出た母は
茂雄の遺体を　取りに走った

この時
妹涼子の顔は　青白く
息は　絶え絶えだった
紘子は　自分の怪我の痛さを忘れ
妹涼子の　手をしっかり握り
必死に　声をかけ続けた

程なくして　母は
砂の付いた　茂雄の遺体を
しっかり抱え　息を切らせ
転げ込むように　家に戻った

母は　寝ている涼子に
覆い被さるようにして
じっと　顔を見た
すると　母を感じた
三歳の　涼子は

――ちゃあちゃん　ぽんぽ　痛いよ！

呻くような　消え入るような声で

Had also been hit
By machine gun fire.
We'll be wiped out if we don't...
She decided to go back to her home.

When she arrived home,
Her mother put Ryoko to bed.
She then returned and ran to pick up Shigeo's body.

At this time,
Her sister Ryoko's face was pale
And she was out of breath.
Hiroko forgot the pain of her own injuries
And held her sister Ryoko's hand tightly.
She continued to call out desperately.

Soon afterwards, her mother,
Holding Shigeo's sand-covered body tightly
And gasping for breath,
Rolled back into the house.

Her mother covered
The sleeping Ryoko
And stared at her face.
Then three-year-old Ryoko,
Who felt her mother...

——My tummy hurts, Chaa-chang!

Ryoko appealed to her mother in a moaning,

母に訴え　こときれた

ちっちゃな涼子の　遺体には
機銃掃射が　お腹を貫通し
太ももには　二カ所の傷があった

── 涼子ちゃん　ごめんね！
── 茂雄ちゃん　ごめんね！

守ろうとした　幼い二人の命に
守られた　母と紘子　二人の命

ありがとう

母は　平成二一年一月二七日
千葉県茂原市の　老人ホームで
静かに　九九年の生涯を閉じた

三七歳の時　三月一〇日の空襲で
夫を亡くし　四人の子を託された

七月七日　疎開した千葉県で
次女涼子　次男茂雄を失った

母は　空襲で亡くした
父のことを
機銃掃射で亡くした

Fading voice and drew her last breath.

Tiny Ryoko's body was found
With a machine gunshot wound
Through her stomach and two wounds on her thighs.

——I'm So Sorry, Ryoko-Chang!
——I'm So Sorry, Shigeo-Chang!

The lives of the two young children they were trying to protect,
In turn, protected their mother and Hiroko.

Thank You!

Her mother passed away on 27 January 2009
At a nursing home in Mobara City, Chiba Prefecture.
She quietly passed away after ninety-nine years of life.

She was thirty-seven years old when her husband was killed
In the air raid on 10 March, leaving her with four children.

On 7 July, in evacuated Chiba Prefecture,
She lost her second daughter Ryoko and her second son Shigeo.

Her mother passed away
Without ever mentioning her husband,
Who was killed in the air raid,

幼い弟妹のことを
口にすることなく
この世を去った

親子で　不安におびえ
怖さに　逃げまどった
あれらの日を
遠い日の思い出として
話すことなど
母にも　紘子にも
できはしない

その日
ホームの母を訪ねた
紘子に向かって

——ありがとう！

と　母が言った
紘子のことを　娘だと
分かっているかのように
はっきりと　言った

——ありがとう！

息を引き取る前の
母の最期の言葉だった

認知症になった母は
だいぶ前から　もう

Or her children,
Who were killed
By machine gun fire.

Neither her nor Hiroko
Would ever be able to
Talk about those days
As distant memories,
When they fled in fear
And anxiety
As mother and children.

Towards Hiroko,
Who visited her mother
At the nursing home that day,

—— Thank you!

So, her mother said,
As if she knew
Hiroko was her daughter.
She said it clearly.

—— Thank you!

Those were her mother's last words
Before she drew her last breath.

Her mother, who has dementia,
Had long since lost track of

娘紘子のことなど
分からなくなっていた
その母が　最後に
紘子に言ってくれたのだろうか……

母は　自分や子どもたちを
見守りつづけてくれた
父に　最後のお礼を
言ったのだろうか……

母と姉の　身代わりになった
涼子と茂雄　幼い二人の
わが子に　最後にお礼を
言ったのだろうか……

それとも　その言葉は
ともに　生き延び
苦楽を　ともにした
紘子に……

――　お母さん　ありがとう！

　　　　　　　　　　　　　合　掌

Her daughter, Hiroko.
She wonders if that
Her mother told Hiroko
For the last time...

Did her mother say a final thank you
To her father
For continuing to look after her
And her children...?

Did the mother thank her two young children,
Ryoko and Shigeo,
Who took the place of her and Hiroko,
In the end...?

Or were those words
Meant for Hiroko,
With whom she survived
And suffered together...?

—— In any case, thank you mother, too!

Gassho (Arigato Gozaimasita)

沈黙をすて

平成二三年四月二〇日
東京高等裁判所での
証人尋問に立った
渡邊紘子は
裁判官の目を
しっかり見据え

―― 空襲は　一家団欒を　奪いました
　　生き残ったことに
　　後ろめたさを拭えない毎日です

―― 幸せを感じられない　わたしです
　　もう一度　涼子ちゃんの歌が聞きたい
　　もう一度　茂雄ちゃんの笑い声を聞きたい

と訴えた

三歳の涼子が
父のいない
家族の寂しさを
慰めようと歌い
姉の紘子に
教えてくれた
お山の杉の子を
法廷で静かに
口ずさんだ

Breaking Silence

On 20 April 2011,
A witness was examined at the Tokyo High Court.
Hiroko Watanabe looked
The judge firmly
In the eye
And told,

—— Air raids deprived us of our family home.
　　Every day I can't shake off the guilt I feel
　　For having survived.

—— I am the one who cannot feel happiness.
　　I wish to hear Ryoko's singing once more.
　　I wish to hear Shigeo's laughter one more time, sincerely.

She made a strong appeal to the judge.

Hiroko quietly hummed in court
The song "Oyama No Sugi No Ko (The Child of the Japanese Cedar)",
Which three-year-old Ryoko sang
To comfort
Her fatherless family.
And Hiroko was taught
The same song
From her younger sister.
Her name was Ryoko-Chang.

六六年間の　沈黙をすて
六六年間を　証言した

——　武器を持たない私たちが　なぜ
　　　あんなに酷い　殺され方をしなければ
　　　ならなかったのか　教えてください

——　父の遺体も　幼い妹や弟の遺体も
　　　どこにあるのか分かりません
　　　私一人の力ではどうすることもできません

と　積年の思いを伝えた

——　私たちの苦しみを　認めてほしい
　　　死者たちに　わびてほしい
　　　慰霊堂を作ってほしい

無念の魂をひろい
心のよりどころとなる
判決がほしいと
思いを結んだ

Hiroko broke her sixty-six years of silence
And testified to the weight of the sixty-six years she had experienced.

—— Please tell us why we, who are unarmed,
    Had to be killed
    In such a disgusting manner.

—— I don't know where my father's body is,
    Or the bodies of my infant sister and brother.
    I cannot do anything about it on my own!

So, she told the judge that she had been thinking about it for years.

—— The state should acknowledge our suffering.
    The State should apologise to the dead.
    The State should build a cenotaph.

She concluded her thoughts
With a desire to have a judgment
That would expand her regretful soul
And provide her with emotional comfort.

第六章　六六年目の　おびえ
──九歳の和子

Chapter 6
The Sixty-Sixth Year of Fear;
Kazuko Was Nine-Year-Old

六六年目の　おびえ

二〇一一年三月一二日
午後一時三〇分
すみだ女性センターには
東北地震による
交通事情　最悪な中を
東京大空襲訴訟原告団の
幾人かが
電車やバスを　乗り継ぎ
歩き　やって来た

テレビを　見ていると
身体が震えて　震えて
どうにもなりません
とくに　気仙沼の
火災現場の映像は
苦しいです

涙があふれて　あふれて……
「お母ちゃん　お母ちゃん！」
と小声で言っている
握り締めている両手には
脂汗がビッショリでした
と　話すのは
鹿嶋市から来た
吉田由美子　六九歳

叔母の背で　助けられた命

The Sixty-Sixth Year of Fear

On 12 March 2011,
1:30 pm.
At the Sumida Women's Center
Due to the Tohoku earthquake
Traffic conditions
At their worst,
The plaintiffs in the Tokyo Air Raid Lawsuit.
By train and bus,
And walked there.

"While watching TV,
I was shaking and trembling.
I couldn't help it.
Especially in Kesennuma
The images of the fire
Made me pain."

"Tears overflowed and overflowed...
'Mum, mum!'
I was whispering.
My hands are clenched in a tight grip.
I was drenched in a greasy sweat."
Yumiko Yoshida told so.
She came From Kashima City.
Aged sixty-nine.

Her life was saved on her aunt's back.

六六年前の東京大空襲の夜
その後の　ねじ曲げられた
彼女の人生が
走馬灯のように
思いだされたと……

彼女が背負わされた
不安や恐怖　おびえが
一挙に呼び覚まされたと……

戦争孤児の思い

私たち
一日でもいいから
震災の人たちのために
街頭に立って
支援のカンパを
集めませんか
私たちだから
何かをしなくては……
と　意を決した声が
第一会議室に響いた

草野和子　七五歳も
また　東京大空襲で
両親と　叔父家族五人
七人を　亡くした

The night of the Tokyo Air Raid,
Sixty-six years ago.
After that, her life was twisted and turned
Her life was
Like a revolving lantern...

Fear and anxiety
She was forced to carry.
Evoked all at once...

Thought of War Orphans

Because it's us,
Even if it's just for one day,
Let's stand on the streets
For the people affected by the disaster
To raise funds for the victims
And collect donations
Because it's us,
We have to do something...
And the voice of determination
Echoed in Conference Room 1.

Kazuko Kusano, Seventy-five years old recalls.
In the Tokyo Air Raid,
She, too, lost her parents and five of her uncle's family
A total of seven people.

小さなお母さん

三月一〇日の　空襲で
両親と　叔父家族を
亡くした
当時九歳の草野和子は
三歳下の弟光夫と一緒に
母のちがう
長女が　産まれたばかりの
長兄の家に　身をよせた

互いが　苦しい生活の中
力を合わせ　命をつないだ
小学生の　和子と光夫の
二人も　学校から帰ると
兄の　プレスの仕事を　手伝った
納期を　まにあわせるために
二人も　徹夜仕事を　手伝った

十分な食事も　十分な睡眠も
できない　混乱した　時代
家族皆が　疲れきっていた
そんなある夜　和子の目が
弟光夫から放れた　とき
光夫の　右人さし指が
機械に挟まれ　切断された

数年後　兄の家を出
弟と二人の生活を　始めた彼女

Little Mother

In the air raid on March 10th,
Kazuko Kusano, who was nine years old at the time
With her brother Mitsuo, who was three years younger than her
They moved in with their eldest brother.
From a different mother,
Her eldest brother's eldest daughter has just been born.
Kazuko's parents and her uncle and his family
Were all lost.

The family has survived
By pulling together in the face of hardship.
Even though they were still in primary school,
Kazuko and Mitsuo helped their older brother
With the press when they came home from school.
To meet deadlines,
They also helped him work all night long.

It was a confusing time,
With not enough food and not enough sleep.
Everyone in the family was exhausted.
One night, when Kazuko's attention was diverted
From her brother Mitsuo,
Mitsuo's right index finger
Was caught in a machine and severed.

Years later, she left her older brother's house
And started a new life with Mitsuo,

兄に心配をかけたくない　一心で
自分の血を売ったこともあったとか
言葉に出来ない苦しみを抱え

弟と身を寄せ合って
生きた
空襲後の　六六年

数々の苦しみを封じ込め
いま　やっと　穏やかな
日々を送っている彼女
だが　彼女の心をいまなお
苦しめていることがあった
仕事中　弟光夫に　指を
落とさせてしまったことだ

高等裁判所での　証人尋問
和子はしっかりとした声で
落ちついて答えていた
気丈な　彼女だった　が
光夫の話になったとき
言葉が詰まり　嗚咽し
肩を震わせ　泣いていた

空襲で　父と母を　亡くした
その夜から　九歳の和子は
六歳の　弟光夫の
小さなお母さんになっていた

茨城県の潮来に　疎開した

Telling how she once sold her own blood
Because she did not want to worry about her older brother.
She had unspeakable pain.

She and her brother
Lived the sixty-six years
After the air raid, they huddled together.

She has finally managed to contain
Her many sufferings
And she is now living a peaceful life.
However, there was one thing
That still torments her.
She let her brother Mitsuo's finger fall off,
While at work.

During witness questioning at the High Court,
Kazuko sounded firm.
She answered calmly.
She was a stout woman,
But when it came to Mitsuo,
She was indeed at a loss for words, sobbing,
Shaking her shoulders and cried.

Since the night her father and mother
Died in the air raid,
Nine-year-old Kazuko has been a little mother
To her six-year-old brother, Mitsuo.

Their Mother, Kazuko and Mitsuo,

母と和子と光夫　親子三人
小学校に入学する
光夫のために
父が用意した　ランドセル
母は　ランドセルを取りに
三月七日　東京に行った
三月一〇日　東京にいた
母は　空襲で死んだ

光夫は　母の帰りを
疑うことなく　待っていた
来る日も　来る日も
バス停にたち続ける光夫
母の帰りを待ち続け
一ヶ月が　過ぎた

光夫の　母を慕い待つ姿に
言い知れぬ　ふびんさ
哀れさを　感じていた
三歳違いの　姉和子
彼女は　この時から
光夫の　小さいお母さんに
なっていたのだ

六六年たち　いまは
弟光夫が　姉和子を
母を慈しむ思いで
見守っている

Were evacuated to Itako, Ibaraki Prefecture.
Father prepared a school backpack for Mitsuo,
Who was about to enter elemental school.
Mother went to Tokyo on 7 March
To pick up his school backpack.
She was in Tokyo on 10 March.
And my mother died in Tokyo Air Raid.

Mitsuo waited without question
For his mother to return home.
Day after day,
Mitsuo stood at the bus stop.
A month has passed
Since he waited for his mother's return.

His sister Kazuko,
Who was three years older than Mitsuo,
Felt an inexpressible sense of inadequacy and pity
When she saw Mitsuo's longing and waiting
For his mother.
She had become Mitsuo's little mother
From this moment on.

Now, sixty-six years later,
Her younger brother Mitsuo
Looks after his sister Kazuko
With the same affection as his mother.

震災によせ

東日本大震災に遭った　方々に
私たちだから　出来ることはと
六六年まえの　戦争孤児たちが
思いを巡らしていた

そして　その思いは
「震災孤児の救済を求める訴え」として
東京大空襲被害者原告団
孤児被害者代表　金田茉莉によって
書かれ　公表され
衆参の議員室に配られた

　——　私たちは、六六年まえの戦争末期、空襲被害によって孤児になった者です。私たちは空からの焼夷爆弾による火の海を逃げまどい、親兄姉が焼け死んでいきました。
　黒焦げになり、身元も分からなくなった遺体の山と遺骨の散乱する焼け野原をさまよいました。
　私たちは、親を失った悲しさと心細さと、これからどうしたら良いのかという不安に押しつぶされていました。
　今回の震災の孤児の方たちは、六六年まえの私たちとまったく一緒でした。今回の被害の様子を知り、あの頃の自分の恐ろしさと不安を一挙に思い出しました。
　本当に苦しいです。

For Disaster

"To the people affected by the Great East Japan Earthquake
What can we do for them?"
War orphans of the Tokyo Air Raid
Were thinking about it.

And their thoughts were published
As an appeal for relief for the orphans of the Great East Japan Earthquake.
Written by Mari Kaneda, a representative of the orphan victim,
In the Tokyo Air Raid Victims Claimants.
It was distributed to the offices of members of the Diet
In both the House of Representatives and the House of Councilors.

—— We are those who were orphaned by air raids at the end of the war 66 years ago. We fled through a sea of fire caused by incendiary bombs from the sky, while our parents and siblings were burnt to death.
We wandered through burnt fields littered with piles of charred and unidentifiable bodies and remains.
We were overwhelmed with sadness and depression at the loss of our parents and anxieties about what to do.
The orphans of this disaster were exactly the same as we were sixty-six years ago. When I learned about the damage this time, I remembered all at once the horror and anxiety I felt back then.
We are really suffering.

―― 政府関係者の方々にお願いです。
　どうか、孤児になった子どもさんたちを第一に救ってください。どの被害者の方も大変なのは分かります。
　でも、親が居なくなるということは、子どもにとっては生きる基盤を失うことです。
　悲しくても心からすがれる存在がなくなるということです。そして、今後、精神的な苦しみや物理的な不自由、有形無形の差別などにさらされていく可能性が大きいのです。

―― 震災から、三週間たち、子どもたちの心は、茫漠自失から本当の苦しみに入っていきます。
　私たち空襲被害孤児で「親と一緒に死ねばよかった」、こう思わなかった孤児はいません。今回の震災孤児たちにこんな思いはさせないでください。
　どうか、孤児たちの生活支援、精神的な支援をまず、お願いします。

六六年前の
戦争孤児たちの
体験から生まれた
心の声が
被災者を思いやる
願いと　祈りの
言葉となって
発せられた

—— We ask government officials.
Please save the orphaned children first and foremost. We understand that it is difficult for all victims.
But to lose a parent is for a child to lose the foundation of life.
It means that even if they are sad, they will no longer have someone to whom they can truly retreat. And there is a great possibility that they will be exposed to mental suffering, physical inconvenience and discrimination, both tangible and intangible, in the future.

—— Three weeks after the disaster, the children's hearts have gone from stupor to real suffering.
There is not an orphan among us air raid orphans who has not thought, "I wish I had died together with my parents". Please don't let the orphans of this disaster feel this way.
Please support the orphans' life and mental support first of all.

The hearts and minds
Of the war orphans born
From their experiences
sixty-six years ago,
They were uttered
As words of wishes
And prayers of compassion
For the victims.

戦争孤児茉莉

学童疎開をしていた
小学校三年の　金田茉莉は
縁故疎開をするため
卒業式で帰宅する
六年生と一緒に
疎開先の宮城県白石から
東北線の夜行列車で帰省した

三月一〇日　朝
子どもたちは
上野駅に　着いた
誰もいない駅　駅の外は
見渡す限りの　焼け野原
この空襲で　金田茉莉は
母と姉と妹を　亡くした
父は　七年前に　病死した
家族を亡くした　茉莉は
戦争孤児になってしまった

独りきりの生活は　厳しく
寂しいものだった
親戚をたらい回しされ
労働のみを課せられる毎日

　——　孤児は働かなければ
　　　食べさせて貰えません

Mari, War Orphan

Mari Kaneda, a third-year elementary school student,
Who had previously been evacuated from her school,
returned home on the overnight train on the Tohoku Line
From Shiroishi, Miyagi Prefecture,
Where she had been evacuated, together with sixth-year students,
Who were returning home for graduation ceremonies
Because they would now be evacuated by nepotism.

On the morning of 10 March,
The children
Arrived at Ueno Station.
The station was empty.
As far as the eye can see, it's a burnt field.
Mari Kaneda lost her mother,
Elder and younger sister in this air raid.
Her father died of illness seven years ago.
Mari lost her family.
She became a war orphan.

Life on her own was hard.
It was lonely.
She was sent from one relative to another.
She was forced to work every day.

—— Orphans have to work, hard.
 If they don't work, they can't afford themselves.

陳述書で　こう書いていた

早く母の処に　逝きたい
病気で倒れて　死ねれば楽になる
と　過重な労働を
受け入れ　生きていた

金田茉莉は　本を出した
戦争孤児たちが　受けた
いわれない　差別を
人間として
関わってもらえなかった
怒りや矛盾を
知らそうと

生き残れなかった
孤児らが　多くいたことを
平和に生きる　今の人たちに
不幸な時代が　あったことを
知らそうと

平和の大切さを
命の大切さを
ともに
考えて欲しいと

人間が　人間として
生きるのに　何が
大切なのかを
考えて欲しいと

In her statement, she said.

She thought, "I can't wait to go to my mother's.
It would be easier if I could just fall ill and die"
So she accepted the overwork
And lived.

Mari Kaneda published a book
To inform war orphans
Of the unspeakable discrimination
They suffered,
Plus the anger and contradictions
Of not being treated
As human beings.

She published a book
To let people know that there were many orphans
Who did not survive,
And that there were unhappy times
For those who live in peace today.

She hoped the readers
To think together
About the importance of peace
And the value of life.

She hoped the readers
To think about
What is important for human beings
To live as human beings.

三月一〇日に　奪われた
幼い者たちの
命が　あったこと
幸いにも　命長らえた
子どもたちが
戦争終結後　生きる為に
どれほど
もがき　苦しんだかを
社会の矛盾と
戦い　続けたかを
知らせなければと
思い出してほしいと

この地球上に　再び
同じ悲しみ　悲劇が
生み出されぬよう
彼女は　パソコンに向かい
今日も　孤児たちの
当時を　知らせねばと
残された　自分の命を
注ぎ込んでいる

復興と平和を

六六年まえの
恐怖におびえながらも

She hoped to remind the readers
Of the lives
Of the little ones
Those were taken on 10 March,
And how even those children
Who were fortunate
Enough to survive
Had to struggle
After the war,
And how they had to fight
Against the contradictions
Of society.

She is at her computer,
Devoting the rest of her life
To write a book
About the orphans' lives
In the hope that the same sadness
And tragedy
Will not be created again
On this planet.

For Reconstruction and Peace

Terrified of the horrors
Of sixty-six years ago,

一歩を踏み出した
戦争孤児たち

いま　理想が　現実となる　奇跡を！
と　平和実現への　祈りをもって

東日本の震災と
自分の被災体験をかさね
六六年の人生と向き合い
被災者の方々を案じている

人が人として誇りをもって
生きていけるよう
人が人への思いやりを
失わぬよう

人が　生きるのに
本当に　必要なもの
大切なことを　見極め
真にあるべき　復興を
平和な生活の存続を
願い　祈っている

The war orphans
Took a step forward.

Now for the miracle of the ideal to become reality!
With prayers for the realization of peace.

They have combined their experiences of the earthquake in eastern Japan
With their own experiences of the Tokyo Air Raids,
And they are facing sixty-six years of their lives
And are concerned for the victims of the disaster.

They hope that people
will not lose their compassion for others
So that they can live proudly
As human beings.

They hope
And pray
For the reconstruction
And continuation
Of peaceful life
As it really should be.

跋文　　弁護士　原田　敬三

　東京大空襲訴訟は、平成十九年三月九日に東京地裁に提訴（原告一一二名——後に一名取下げ）され、第二次訴訟は平成二十年三月十日に原告二十名で提訴（第一次訴訟に併合）した。求める内容は国が救済しなかったことの慰謝料請求と空襲被害の調査・謝罪、そして国立追悼施設の建立である。
　原告団は、空襲当時十歳前後で父母を失った疎開児童などが多数を占める。
　平成十九年五月から二十一年五月まで、専門家証人四名（早乙女勝元、野田正彰、池谷好治、内藤光博）、原告本人十二名の証拠調べが行われた。
　平成二十一年十二月十四日　判決言渡となり、「原告らの請求をいずれも棄却する。」との原告全面敗訴の不当判決であった。
　原告ら一三一名のうち、一一三名が同年十二月二十五日に控訴した。
　控訴審では四人の原告本人が証言した。

　米軍による東京への空襲は昭和二十年三月十日をはじめに、四月五月と大規模に三回くり返され、死者は推定十万五千人以上にのぼった。東京市街地の六割が焦土と化した。この直接被害状況は早乙女勝元氏の『東京大空襲』（岩波新書）などに詳しい。成人男子の大半が戦場に召集され、女性や子どもなど社会的弱者が空襲被害者となった。辛くも生き残った人の多くは、孤児となったり、障害を被ったりしていた。戦争孤児らは全国で三万人以上と言われた。

Background Explanation by Keizo Harada (Lawyer)

The Tokyo Air Raid Lawsuit was filed in the Tokyo District Court on 9 March 2007 (112 plaintiffs - one later withdrew), and the second lawsuit was filed on 10 March 2008 with 20 plaintiffs (joined with the first lawsuit). The content of the lawsuit is a demand for compensation for the State's failure to provide relief, an investigation and apology for the air raid damage, and the erection of a national memorial facility.

The majority of the plaintiffs are children who were around ten-years old at the time of the air raid and who lost their parents.

From May 2007 to May 2009, four expert witnesses (Katsumoto Saotome, Masaaki Noda, Yoshiharu Iketani and Mitsuhiro Naito) and 12 plaintiffs themselves were examined for evidence.

On 14 December 2009, a judgment was handed down, stating that "The claims of the plaintiffs are all dismissed." The judgment was unjust and the plaintiffs lost the case entirely.

Of the 131 plaintiffs, 113 appealed on 25 December of the same year. Four plaintiffs testified at the appeal hearing.

US air raids on Tokyo were repeated three times on a massive scale, beginning on 10 March 1945 and continuing in April and May, with an estimated death toll of over 105,000. Sixty percent of the urban area of Tokyo was scorched to ashes. The direct damage is detailed in Katsumoto Saotome's *Tokyo Air Raid* (Iwanami Shinsho) and other books. Most of the adult male population was called up to the battlefield, while women, children and other socially vulnerable people became victims of the air raid. Many of those who narrowly survived were orphaned or disabled. It was estimated that there were more than 30,000 war orphans in the country.

昭和三十年、経済白書が「もはや戦後は終わった」と述べて、多くの国民がその思いを共感した時、「まだ戦後が来ていない」とする国民が少なからずいた。
　空襲被災者らであり、本件原告らである。
　東京大空襲裁判の目的は、国家賠償請求を内容としているが、国家による戦争被災者の救済は行われるべきであった、ということに尽きる。放置されたままの戦争孤児の彼女彼らが訴訟原告団の中心であり、家を失った事を理由とする原告は四名だった。六十六年の時を経た今、原告自らの手でようやく救済立法を掲げた国会への働きかけが始まった。

　裁判手続きでは、事実を裁判官に提供し、裁判官は提供された事実の上に、法律を適用させ、その「計測」した結果を公式な判断として、当事者と世間に発表する。本件にあっては当てはめるべき具体的法律がいまだない。あるのは憲法のみである。
　「あなたの証言は、裁判では本人尋問と言い、公式な記録として残るんです。」との弁護士らの語りかけに、原告一人ひとりが意を決し、心持ちを大きく切り替え尋問に臨んだ。証言する原告は誰もが一応に、裁判官は理解してくれるものと確信に近い信頼を持って法廷に臨んでいた。
　「裁判官は人格識見に優れ、正義の判断をされる偉い人」。多くの国民に浸透しているこの素朴な信頼は一審裁判官により裏切られた。
　日本の司法史上初めて孤児らは証言台に立ち、東京大空襲がもたらした自身の人生被害をわずか三十分ほどに凝縮して明らかにした。
　浅見洋子が向き合った最初の原告は石川智恵子さんで

In 1965, when the Economic White Paper stated that the post-war period was over, and many people shared this sentiment, there were still a small number of people who felt that the post-war period had not yet arrived.

They were the air raid victims and the plaintiffs in this case.

The purpose of the Tokyo Air Raid Trial is to claim state compensation, but it is all about the relief of war victims by the state, which should have taken place. The war orphans, who had been neglected, were at the heart of the plaintiffs in the case, and there were four plaintiffs who claimed to have lost their homes. Now, sixty-six years later, the plaintiffs themselves have finally begun to lobby the National Assembly for relief legislation.

In court proceedings, the facts are provided to the judge, who applies the law to the facts provided and announces his/her "measured" result as an official judgement to the parties and the public. In this case, there is still no specific law to apply. There is only the Constitution.

"Your testimony will be called an examination in court and will be part of the official record." The lawyers' words made each and every one of the plaintiffs determined to testify, and they changed their minds and went through with the questioning. All of the plaintiffs came to court with a sense of confidence that the judge would understand their testimony.

"The judge is a great man of character and insight, a judge of justice." This simple trust, which permeates many people, was betrayed by the judge at the first instance.

For the first time in Japan's judicial history, orphans took the stand and revealed the damage to their own lives caused by the Tokyo air raids in just 30 minutes.

The first plaintiff Yoko Asami faced was Chieko Ishikawa. She witnessed Chieko's story during interviews with her husband Keizo Harada, who used their home as a meeting place, which led her to enter the lives of the plaintiffs, and this poetry book was born.

The children, who were non-combatants and were supposed to be the

あった。自宅を打合せの場にした夫原田敬三の聞き取りで智恵子さんの物語に立ち会ったのが、原告らの人生に踏み込むきっかけとなり、この詩集が誕生した。

　非戦闘員であり、戦争責任から最も遠いはずの子どもらは、ある日突然両親の死と直面した。「空襲でおまえの両親は死んだ」と疎開先で告げられた者。親の死を知らされず、その後の人生に空洞を抱き続けた者も多くいた。

　六十六年前の孤児らは、両親の庇護を失い、人生最大の被害を被りながら、国の救済対象にされることなく、放置され無視され続けた。

　空襲被害を語る時「十万人死んだ戦争があった」と過去の話に集約してはならない。また、「自分たちも空襲では苦労した」と、安易な同等化や同一視で終わらせてはいけない。放置の果ての、その後の孤児らの人生を知ることは、我々のせめてもの義務ではなかろうか。

　ちなみに、彼ら彼女らに国家が取った施策は唯一、『浮浪者狩り』といわれる理由なき収容と虐待であった。当時の新聞を読むと、孤児らは、はじめは憐れみの対象として、ついで戦後の風物詩として、つぎに取り締まり対象として、社会が向き合っていた事が窺われる。「上野の孤児に食べ物をあげないでください」と呼びかける政府の閣議決定（一九四八年九月七日）を伝える新聞記事はあっても、孤児救済のキャンペーンは世論の関心対象とはならず、ヨーロッパのような救済立法は制定されなかった。

　その原因には、複数の要因が絡んでいる。米軍が自分たちの加害の生き証人の存在の表面化を恐れ占領期間中（一九五二年まで）民間人被害の存在をあいまいにしたこと、無差別爆撃・空爆をその後の世界戦争の主たる手

furthest away from war responsibility, were suddenly confronted one day with the death of their parents. Some were told in evacuation centers that their parents had died in the air raid. Many were not informed of their parents' deaths and continued to feel a void in their lives.

Sixty-six years ago, orphans lost the protection of their parents and suffered the greatest damage of their lives, yet they were neglected and ignored by the state without being targeted for relief.

When talking about the damage caused by the air raids, it should not be reduced to the past, saying that "There was a war in which 100,000 people died". Nor should it end with easy equivocation or identification, such as "We had a hard time in the air raids too". It is our duty, at the very least, to know the lives of the orphans afterwards, at the end of their neglect.

Incidentally, the only measures taken by the state against them were detention and abuse without reason, known as "vagrant hunting". Reading the newspapers of the time, it is clear that orphans were first treated with pity, then as a post-war tradition, and then as a target for crackdowns by the society. Despite newspaper articles reporting on the government's cabinet decision (7 September 1948) calling on the public not to give food to orphans in Ueno, the campaign to save orphans was not the subject of public concern, and no relief legislation was enacted, as in Europe.

Multiple factors contributed to this. (i) The fact that the US military obscured the existence of civilian casualties during the occupation (until 1952) for fear of bringing to light living witnesses to their own perpetration; (ii) The desire to maintain the legitimacy of the choice of indiscriminate bombing and aerial bombing as the main means of subsequent world war (see Shinichi Arai, *A History of Air Raids,* Iwanami Shinsho). In Japan, the military state policy of protecting minors as a small nation (Sho Kokumin) in the war effort collapsed with the defeat of the war; the Ministry of Health and Welfare (Kosei Sho), which was established to provide relief, had inherited the structure of the Ministry of Home Affairs (Naimu Sho)

段として選択したことの正当性を保ち続けたいとしたこと（荒井信一著『空爆の歴史』（岩波新書）に詳しい）、日本では、少国民として未成年者を戦争戦力として保護していた軍事国家政策が敗戦により崩壊したこと、救済に当たるべく発足した厚生省が内務省の体質を引き継ぎ歴史的制約があったこと、国民が我が事に追われ弱者を思う余裕がなかったこと、更に、新憲法が制定されたがその実が伴っていなかったこと、などが挙げられる。

憲法学的には、今回の裁判で「孤児の救済が憲法上当然の国家義務であり、孤児らの権利である」事が、内藤光博教授（専修大学。地裁意見書）・青井未帆教授（学習院大学。高裁意見書）の挑戦により解明された。

家族が崩壊し、自らの生計を立てなければならない孤児の辛苦は生涯続いた。

石川智恵子さん当時六歳は、三月十日に兄弟二人と両親を失い、残された兄姉との三人は親戚にばらばらに引きとられた。親を失った兄弟が共に生きることをこの国は許さなかった。小学生の彼女が姉に会いに行く姿を想像すると涙が出る。智恵子さんは判決直後に亡くなられた。

幸一は証言しなかった原告がモデルである。満一歳の時、空襲で父を失い、五人の子を育てる母は生活保護を受け、世間の偏見に晒された。

吉田由美子は三歳の時被災した。東京〜高崎〜東京〜新潟（糸魚川）、さらに別の親戚にやられ、最後の家で高校卒業までの十二年間差別と虐待を受け続けた。母の所在を知りたいと行動をおこした時、彼女はすでに齢五十四歳を数えていた。

「八歳のマサヒロ」は浅見洋子の実兄が空襲で被った荷

and was subject to historical restrictions; the people were so preoccupied with their own affairs that they had no time to think of the weak; and the new Constitution, which was enacted, had no real substance. The new constitution was enacted, but it was not accompanied by a new constitution.

In terms of constitutional law, the court case showed that "relief for orphans is a natural state duty under the Constitution and a right of the orphans", according to the challenges by Prof. Mitsuhiro Naito (Senshu University, District Court Opinion) and Prof. Miho Aoi (Gakushuin University, High Court Opinion).

The orphans' hardship of having to earn their own livelihoods after their families collapsed continued throughout their lives.

Chieko Ishikawa, then aged six, lost her two brothers and two sisters and her parents on 10 March, and her remaining three siblings were taken in by relatives. The country did not allow siblings who had lost their parents to live together. When I imagine her as a primary school student going to see her older sister, I cry. Chieko passed away shortly after the verdict.

Koichi was modelled on a plaintiff who did not testify. At the age of one, she lost her father in and the air raid and her mother, who was raising five children, was on welfare and subjected to public prejudice.

Yumiko Yoshida was affected by the disaster when she was three years old. She was beaten by relatives from Tokyo - Takasaki - Tokyo - Niigata (Itoigawa) and then another relative, and continued to suffer discrimination and abuse in her last home for twelve years until she graduated from high school. She was already fifty-four years old when she took action to find out where her mother was.

"Eight-Year-Old Masahiro" is a requiem from the perspective of younger sister, the author of this book Yoko Asami', who identified the weight of the burden her own brother suffered in the air raids as the starting point for his subsequent life of alcoholic and early death.

Kazuko Watanabe, born in 1933, suffered the air raid on Tokyo at the age

の重さを、その後のアルコール依存症と早世の人生の原点と見極めた妹の視線の鎮魂歌である。
　渡邊紘子（一九三三年生まれ）は、十二歳で東京大空襲に遭い、避難した千葉で、人家を避け海岸線を逃げるさなか機銃掃射で、生後四ケ月の弟と三歳の妹を死なせた。証言準備の中で、彼女は母が、夫の死・二人の幼子の死を終世語らなかったことの重さを理解し、亡き母への共感を深めた。（非武装の民間人を狙い撃ちすることは国際法違反の戦争犯罪である。）
　草野和子さんは満九歳で被災。茨城県潮来に縁故疎開中、両親を失う。身を寄せた兄家族（プレス工場経営）との極貧生活の中、三歳下の弟が指切断事故を起こし、これを自分のせいと責めつづけている。その後の自身の売血生活も当然のことと述べる活動家が、はじめて辛く厳しい思いを吐露した。
　読者には、理解するよりも、共感することを願う。

of 12 and was evacuated to Chiba, where her four-month-old brother and three-year-old sister were killed by machine-gun fire as they fled along the coastline, avoiding human habitation. In the course of preparing her testimony, she understood the gravity of the fact that her mother had not spoken about the death of her husband and two young children for the rest of her life, and her sympathy for her mother deepened. (Targeting unarmed civilians is a war crime in breach of international law.)

Kazuko Kusano was affected at the age of nine. She lost her parents when she was evacuated to Itako, Ibaraki Prefecture. While living in extreme poverty with her brother and his family (who ran a press factory), her younger brother, who was three years younger than her, had his finger amputated, which she blames on herself. For the first time, the activist, who describes her own subsequent life of bloodsellling as a matter of course, reveals her painful and harsh feelings.

We hope readers will empathize rather than understand.

あとがき

「金子秀夫氏にご紹介頂き、はじめてお電話します、鈴木比佐雄です。」と、私のもとに一本の電話が入りました。コールサック社が企画している『大空襲三一〇人詩集』への参加を呼びかけるものでした。荒川区南千住で産声を上げた二人の縁が共鳴し、参加へのチャレンジをお約束しました。

　そして一気に書き上げましたのが、詩「独りぽっちの人生(せいかつ)」でした。

　原爆や空襲の惨さ、戦争の酷さを観念的に理解しているに過ぎない私には、戦争反対との声も観念的に過ぎず、いま一歩、心からの声になっていない自分に反発し、もどかしさを拭えないでいました。

　そうした折り、東京大空襲訴訟原告団のお一人で、証人尋問に立たれる事になった石川智恵子さんの人生を、智恵子さんと夫敬三の傍らでお茶を入れながら耳にした私に、一つの思いが芽生えました。

　智恵子さんが話されるその後の生活苦に、「あっ、これが戦争なのだ！」と思ったのです。

　一九四五年三月一〇日の東京大空襲の惨事は、多くの方々が語り伝えております。ですが、今、私が耳にしている石川智恵子さんの話は違いました。当時六歳だった少女が、この日を境に歩まされた人生でした。大きくねじ曲げられた人生を背負い生きた智恵子さんに戦後は来ていませんでした。不安と孤独はあの日のままだったのです。ねじ曲げられた人生に、貧しさと差別と言う社会の非情が追い打ちをかけていました。

　戦争体験を持たない私にできること、それは戦後を持

Afterwards by Yoko Asami

"This is Hisao Suzuki, calling for the first time after being introduced by Mr. Hideo Kaneko." I received a phone call. It was an invitation to participate in an anthology *The Great Air Raid Poems by 310 Poets*, which was being edited by Coal Sack Inc. The two of us, who were born in Minami Senju, Arakawa Ward, resonated with each other, and I promised to take up the challenge of participating.

Then, I wrote the poem "A Sole, Daily Life" at once.

I had only a conceptual understanding of the horrors of the atomic bombings and air raids and the cruelty of war, and my opposition to war was only conceptual, and I could not shake off the feeling of frustration and rebellion that my voice was not coming from the heart.

Then, as I sat beside Chieko Ishikawa and her husband Keizo, making tea and listening to the life story of her, one of the plaintiffs in the Tokyo air raid lawsuit, who was to stand as a witness. A thought came to me.

The hardships that Chieko told me about afterwards made me think "Oh, this is war!".

Many people have recounted the horrific Tokyo Air Raid on 10 March 1945. But the story of Chieko Ishikawa that I am hearing now is different. It was the life of a girl who was six-years old at the time, and was forced from that day. The post-war period did not come for Chieko, who lived with a life that was greatly twisted. Her anxiety and loneliness remained as they were on that day. Her twisted life was followed by the cruelty of a society of poverty and discrimination.

I realised that what I could do, as the one who has no war experience, was to tell the story of Chieko's life, which has not been lived since the war.

Two years after the publication of *The Great Air Raid Poem by 310 Poets*, on 10 March 2009, I received a phone call at my place of work. It was from

たない智恵子さんの人生を伝える事なのではと思い至りました。

『大空襲三一〇人詩集』が二〇〇九年三月一〇日に出版された二年後、私の勤め先に一本の電話が入りました。鈴木比佐雄氏からでした。
「墨田区立文化中学校の深見響子先生に、電話をしてあげてください。」とのことでした。書店でこの詩集を買い求めた深見教諭は、美術の卒業作品に絵本の制作を考え、詩「独りぽっちの人生」をそのテーマにしたいとコールサック社に連絡があり、私の了解を得たい旨の申し出がなされたのでした。
　二〇一一年五月、「生徒たちの作品を直接見て欲しい」と、深見先生が絵本と詩の感想文を持って飯田橋の事務所に来てくださいました。

　三月一一日、東日本を襲った地震と津波によって壊滅した市町村の姿を、テレビ画面で目にした私は、空襲で焼け野原となった東京を連想していました。「六六年前と同じ過ちが、繰り返されてはいけない。」と直感した私は、文化中学校の卒業生お一人おひとりの絵本や感想文に改めて力を頂き、吉田由美子さん・草野和子さん・渡邊紘子さん・金田茉莉さんたちの人生にと詩作活動を進めました。
　そして、鈴木比佐雄氏の後押しを得、詩集『独りっぽちの人生――東京大空襲により心をこわされた子たち』が、上梓されました。

　平和実現への祈り　理想が現実となる奇跡を！　と…

Mr. Hisao Suzuki.

"Please call Ms. Kyoko Fukami, a teacher at Bunka Junior High School in Sumida Ward, Tokyo." He said. After buying a copy of the book at a bookshop, Ms. Kyoko Fukami contacted Coal Sack Publishing Company, and asked for my permission to use the poem "A Sole, Daily Life" as the theme for her students' graduation work.

In May 2011, Ms. Fukami came to my office in Idabashi with picture books and a poems, saying that she wanted to see the students' works in person.

On 11 March, when I saw on TV the cities, towns and villages devastated by the earthquake and tsunami that hit eastern Japan, I was reminded of Tokyo, which had been burnt to the ground in the air raid. I felt that "The same mistakes of sixty-six years ago must not be repeated." I was inspired by the picture books and essays of each of the graduates of Bunka Junior High School, and I began to write poems about the lives of Yumiko Yoshida, Kazuko Kusano, Hiroko Watanabe and Mari Kaneda.

With the support of Mr. Hisao Suzuki, Poetry collection: *A Sole, Daily Life; The Struggling Children of the Tokyo Air Raids* was published.

Pray for the peace, the miracle of an ideal becoming reality!

I hope that the reconstruction of eastern Japan after the earthquake will be planned and realised in a way that values the climate and sensibility of the Japanese people, so that it will become a source of strength and pride for the Japan of tomorrow, and I pray that the reconstruction will be based on the lessons of the lives of air raid victims who were forgotten sixty-six years ago, and that it will be close to the hearts of those who are still living with the damage of sixty-six years ago. We pray that you will be close to them.

I would like to thank Ms. Kyoko Fukami and her students at Sumida-ku (Sumida Ward) Bunka Junior High School, Mr. Hisao Suzuki, Mr. Kenichi Saso for proofreading and review, Mr. Yugo Chiba for typesetting, and Ms. Ayumi Akutsu and Ms. Shizuka Sugiyama for binding. I would like to ex-

東日本の震災復興が、明日の日本の力となり誇りとなるよう、日本人の日本人たる風土と感性を大切にした計画がなされ実現される事を願うとともに、六六年前に忘れられた空襲被害者の方々の人生を教訓にした復興と、六六年前の被害を、いま尚、背負い生きておられる方々の心に寄り添って頂けるよう祈ります。

　墨田区立文化中学校の深見響子先生と教え子の皆様、鈴木比佐雄氏をはじめ、校正・校閲の佐相憲一氏、組版の千葉勇吾氏、装丁の亜久津歩氏と杉山静香氏の皆様、ありがとうございました。私に心を開き、苦しくも強く生きられた東京大空襲訴訟原告団のお一人おひとりに感謝と敬意を捧げます。

　最後に、石川智恵子様のご冥福を心からお祈り申し上げます。(合掌)

　　　　　　　　　　　　　　二〇一一年六月二二日
　　　　　　　　　　　　　　浅見洋子

press my gratitude and respect to each and every one of the plaintiffs in the Tokyo Air Raid Litigation, who opened their hearts to me and lived their lives painfully but strongly.

Lastly, I would like to express my heartfelt prayers for the repose of the soul of late Chieko Ishikawa. (Arigato Gozaimasita, Gassho)

22 June 2011
Yoko Asami

日英詩集に寄せるご挨拶

　私が二〇一一年七月に刊行した『独りぼっちの人生(せいかつ)——東京大空襲により心をこわされた子たち』は在庫が無くなり、国内のみならず海外の東京大空襲の研究者たちからも増刷の要望が続いていた。そこでコールサック社代表の鈴木比佐雄氏に相談したところ、「英語に翻訳して、世界の人びとにも読まれる日英詩集を刊行しませんか」という提案があった。しばらく考えたが、私はその提案を受け入れた。翻訳には推薦のあったソマイア・ラミシュ、C・S・ルイス、D・M・トマス、ウィルフリッド・ウィルスン・ギブスンら海外詩人の翻訳をされている翻訳家・詩人の岡和田晃氏にお願いすることとした。日本語と英語の対訳の編集になっており、とても読み易く学生たちにも勧めたい。本書を通して東京大空襲の戦災孤児たちの経験が世界の人たちの心に伝わって下さることを心から願っている。

　増刷を勧めて下った皆様、本書を実際に製作して下さったコールサック社の鈴木比佐雄氏とスタッフの皆様、翻訳をして下さった岡和田晃様に心より感謝の思いをお伝え致します。

　　　　　　　　　　　　　　　二〇二五年一月
　　　　　　　　　　　　　　　浅見洋子

Greetings to the revised Japanese & English poetry collection

The original book, *The Struggling Children of the Tokyo Air Raids,* which I published in July 2011, ran out of stock, and there were many requests for reprints from researchers of the Tokyo Air Raids both in Japan and overseas. When I consulted with Mr. Hisao Suzuki, the representative of Coal Sack Publishing Company, he suggested that translating the book into English and publishing a collection of Japanese-English poems that could be read by people around the world. After thinking about it for a while, I accepted the proposal and recommendation. I decided to ask Mr. Akira Okawada, a translator and poet who translates the works of Somaia Ramish, C.S.Lewis, D.M.Thomas, Wilfrid Wilson Gibson, and other global authors, to translate the book. The book is edited in Japanese and English and is easy to read and I would recommend it to students. I sincerely hope that the experiences of the war orphans of the Tokyo air raids will be conveyed to the hearts of people around the world through this book.

I would like to express my sincere thanks to everyone who recommended the revised edition, to Mr. Hisao Suzuki and the staff of the Coal Sack Publishing Company who actually produced this book, and to Mr. Akira Okawada for English translation.

January 2025
Yoko Asami

著者略歴

浅見　洋子（あさみ　ようこ）

一九四九年生まれ。和洋女子大学卒。

［著書］
詩集『歩道橋』（けやき書房）
詩集『交差点』（けやき書房）
詩集『隅田川の堤』（けやき書房）
詩画集『母さんの海』（世論時報社）
詩集『マサヒロ兄さん』（けやき書房）
詩集『もぎ取られた青春』（花伝社）
詩集『水俣のこころ』（花伝社）
詩集『独りぽっちの人生（せいかつ）―東京大空襲により心をこわされた子たち』（コールサック社）
『大空襲三一〇人詩集』（コールサック社）、『鎮魂詩四〇四人集』（コールサック社）に参加。
現在、全国空襲被害者連絡協議会の運動に携わっている。

現住所　〒145-0062　東京都大田区北千束1-33-2

Yoko Asami's Biography.

Born in 1949. Graduated from Wayo Women's University.

List of main publications are as below,
Poetry collection: *Pedestrian Bridge*, Keyaki Shobo.
Poetry collection: *Crossroads*, Keyaki Shobo.
Poetry collection: *Sumida River's bank*, Keyaki Shobo.
Poetry and art collection: *Mother's Sea*, Seoron Jihosha.
Poetry collection: *Brother Masahiro*, Keyaki Shobo.
Poetry collection: *The Youth That Was Ripped Away*, Kadensha.
Poetry collection: *The Heart of Minamata*, Kadensha.
Poetry collection: *The Struggling Children of the Tokyo Air Raids*, Coal Sack Publishing Company.
Participated in the anthologies: *The Great Air Raid Poems by 310 Poets*, Coal Sack Publishing Company, *Elegies by 444 Poets,* Publishing Company.

Currently, she participated the movement of Liason Council of Air-Raid Victims of Japan.

Current address: 1-33-2, Kita Senzoku, Ota-ku, Tokyo 145-0062, Japan.

日英詩集　独りぽっちの人生(せいかつ)
——東京大空襲により心をこわされた子たち

Yoko Asami's Poetry Collection In Japanese & English
The Struggling Children of the Tokyo Air Raids

2025 年 1 月 23 日初版発行
編著者　　浅見洋子
訳　者　　岡和田晃
編集・発行者　鈴木比佐雄
発行所　株式会社 コールサック社
〒 173-0004　東京都板橋区板橋 2-63-4-209
電話 03-5944-3258　FAX 03-5944-3238
suzuki@coal-sack.com　http://www.coal-sack.com
郵便振替　00180-4-741802
印刷管理　（株）コールサック社　制作部

装幀　松本菜央

落丁本・乱丁本はお取り替えいたします。
ISBN978-4-86435-641-1　C0092　￥2000E

Yoko Asami's Poetry Collection In Japanese & English
The Struggling Children of the Tokyo Air Raids

Copyright © 2025 by Yoko Asami
English translation by Akira Okawada
Published by Coal Sack Publishing Company

Coal Sack Publishing Company
2-63-4-209 Itabashi Itabashi-ku Tokyo 173-0004 Japan
Tel: (03)5944-3258 / Fax: (03)5944-3238
suzuki@coal-sack.com　http://www.coal-sack.com
President: Hisao Suzuki

墨田区立文花中学校
第十二期生　卒業制作

Sumida-ku (Sumida Ward) Bunka Junior High School,
12th Graduation Works
(The Original Illustrations Inspired From This Book)

阿部俊真

井野若桜

市村安莉沙

金谷太一

斉藤希実

鈴木実花

髙見澤夏奈

武田寛昭

富山昌美

松島慶

松本澪

百瀬拓海

安田美桜

吉岡瑞生

吉成将太

渡邉尚美

池田彩乃

生駒貴吉

石川友理江

加藤秀門

熊﨑桃子

倉林育生

小林弥優

佐藤哲平

宍戸優太

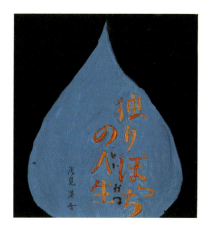

柴田裕翔

竹内耀

田中輝

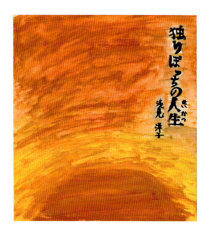

田中勇祐

德田拓人

富川莉緒

橋本侑樹

三好真央

村川奈美

山岸須美香

山田健太

吉田博貴

吉野聡浩

佐久間颯万

林大樹

村山睦

天坂龍依

甘利哲也

石井みなみ

太田彩乃

太田彩乃

垣花航介

神﨑嵩志

佐瀬正史

篠原健太

杉本春香

谷島優希

富岡茜

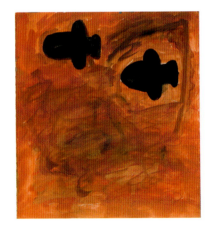

鳥居本莉緒

長峯芳雄

長峯芳雄

萩野茂樹

増田拓未

南亜沙美

山岸江里奈

Y. S